Strange phantoms of the night

- Who was setting off the false alarms that were running the firemen ragged? Who or what? Nancy Jo thought she knew. She had seen a white phantom blob glide through the night. And she had to find it because she herself had been accused of causing the false alarms!

- Chuck didn't like the Scottish Islands. The days were rainy, foggy, and full of ominous clouds. Besides, it was boring there. At least until the night he and his friend Sandy climbed up to the lonely ruined castle and saw the Ghost of Black John. But why was the ghost sending signals across the water?

- When their car broke down, Jim, Milly, and their little brother Buddy were stranded in a strange, barren countryside. The only building in sight was the Old Stone Fort, a ruin full of ancient graves, eerie Indian legends—and a pair of huge luminous eyes that wandered through the night.

GHOST STORIES

Edited by A.L. Furman

AN ARCHWAY PAPERBACK
Published by POCKET BOOKS • NEW YORK

"The Ghost of Old Stone Fort" reprinted from *Twelve/Fifteen*, copyright, ©, 1957, by Pierce and Washabaugh; "Valley of No Return" reprinted from *Twelve/Fifteen*, copyright, ©, 1960, by Pierce and Washabaugh; "Mystery of the Ghost Junk" reprinted from *Twelve/Fifteen*, copyright, ©, 1960, by Pierce and Washabaugh.

Ghost Stories was originally published under the title *Teen-Age Ghost Stories*

An Archway Paperback published by
POCKET BOOKS, a division of Simon & Schuster, Inc.
1230 Avenue of the Americas, New York, N.Y. 10020

Copyright © 1961 by A. L. Furman

Published by arrangement with Lantern Press, Inc.

ISBN: 0-671-52525-5

First Pocket Books printing February, 1964

20 19 18 17 16 15 14 13

AN ARCHWAY PAPERBACK and colophon are trademarks of Simon & Schuster, Inc.

Printed in the U.S.A.

IL 5+

To all spooks, phantoms and ghosts

Contents

GHOST STORIES

Ghost Alarm

CARL HENRY RATHJEN

MOANNNNN . . .

The heaviness of it shook the June night, shook the house and wakened Nancy-Jo with a start. She lay quivering. Her brown eyes stared at the armless form draped on the chair, until she recognized it as the gown she'd worn to the high-school prom. Her gaze darted toward curtains cringing from the open window as that wavering moan suddenly filled the chill night. It must be the biggest ghost there ever was!

No, silly, she chided herself, flinging back the blanket when she heard dogs barking and saw buttery chips of light appear in neighboring houses. It was the town's fire horn, summoning volunteers from beds for the seventh consecutive night.

Then, as the moaning choked off, she heard a strange rustling in the bushes beside the house. That couldn't be someone already answering the alarm. Not that fast at this hour. Besides, there was no

1

path through that tangled jungle and, whoever it was, was going away from the fire station!

The horn gave another full-throated blast.

Nancy-Jo swung her feet into jeans draped over boots. She'd have to hurry if she was going to make it to the fire station ahead of Dave Cummins, who refused to believe that a girl whose father had been in the trucking business could drive Number Two rig as well as a man. She tugged the jeans over shortie pajamas, then, stabbing into a light jacket on her way to the door, she glanced out the window . . . and glimpsed a white blob floating rapidly through the bushes!

She sucked her breath, paused rigidly, trying to summon nerve to lean out and see what *that* was. Had she seen it, or wasn't she awake yet? The horn moaned urgently again. Bursting into the hall she saw a sudden sliver of light gleam under the bedroom door of her uncle and aunt who had adopted her.

"Nan!" Uncle Jim called sharply.

"I'm on my way!" she replied, running toward the stairs.

"Dress warmly!" Aunt Sue shrilled.

Nancy-Jo shivered, thinking of that white phantom. She wished she dared wait for her elderly uncle. But there would be other volunteers converging on the station. She wouldn't be alone in the night, she hoped.

On the front porch she braced to a stop, seeking that white blob, then remembered it had been going away from the street. She raced down the steps, cutting across the lawn toward the pole on the corner. The edge of her wide gaze watched the dark mass of bushes to her right.

She dashed through the dim aura of the redlight on the pole and, between moans from the fire tower a block ahead, heard an automobile starter growl. Somewhere else a motor roared. In the night behind her, footsteps pounded. She didn't look back to see if they were human, just ran faster as the bleating fire horn seemed to push the night against her straining face.

Floodlights suddenly poured a pool of welcome glare over the ramp of the fire station. One set of the big doors yawned open and with a snorting rumble Number One rig nosed out with lanky Joe Hadley, the town's part-time paid fireman, at the wheel. He'd wait sixty seconds from the first sound of the alarm, then roll with whatever volunteers had arrived. Nancy-Jo, or Dave Cummins, would follow with Number Two thirty seconds later. Volunteers who came in from farther out in town would get the location from the blackboard, or swing their cars in trailing pursuit of the rigs.

Tingling fingers of fear, or was it the white blob, prodded between Nancy-Jo's shoulders as she made it into the bright safety of the floodlights. Joe Hadley's face seemed more cadaverous than ever as his head swiveled on a scrawny neck.

"You look like the flying artiste of the circus. It's Box Twelve, your corner, Nan. Did you see what it was?"

Nancy-Jo shook her head, knowing he referred

3

to the fire. There was no time to explain what she had seen, or had she imagined it? Grabbing a blue cap from the rack—drivers didn't wear helmets—she swept her brown hair under it and was just settling behind Number Two's wheel when Dave Cummins arrived on the run. He hadn't been in bed. His sandy hair wasn't tousled and he still had on the grey slacks and white coat he'd worn to the prom. Had their argument bothered him that much? Or, Nancy-Jo wondered with a tinge of jealousy, had he gone back to the prom after taking her home?

"You got here fast," he called up to her.

"Thank you," she said coolly, pulling the lanyard to open the door before the rig. "Maybe you won't believe everything you read about volunteers in textbooks."

Dave was majoring in fire science up at State Tech, and during the weeks he'd been home on summer vacation he'd been too outspokenly critical of volunteer fire departments. Nancy-Jo wished she hadn't made the "dig," but there was no time to apologize.

Big Sam Tyson, hardware dealer and local fire chief, was swinging up beside Joe Hadley on Number One. He looked hollow-eyed, but his voice boomed.

"Follow along, Nan. It's close enough for late-comers to run another block or so."

Dave and pudgy, sourfaced old Mort Garner, who ran the feed store, leaped aboard Number Two along with three other volunteers. Nancy-Jo gunned out over the ramp with a rising wail of siren. Driving back toward home her eyes searched for smoke, for flame, and for signs of a white phantom.

Number One pulled up by the alarm box on the corner pole. Chief Tyson, Joe, and helmeted heads looked around for the person who had pulled it. There was no one. Obviously another false alarm. Or was it a ghost alarm, Nancy-Jo wondered, stopping Number Two so the headlights probed the dark bushes. Nothing. Then she saw her lean Uncle Jim in his car because he could never make it fast enough to ride a rig to a fire. She called to him.

"When you got the car out, did you see anyone . . . or anything?"

He shook his head wonderingly. Dave stared at her, so did Chief Tyson and his red-headed son, Rick, the town constable.

"Speak up, Nan," said the chief. "Do you know something about this false alarm?"

Nancy-Jo was going to answer "Yes." Then she saw the green smears on Dave's white coat as he unbuckled his turn-out. Had he been pushing through those bushes? She suddenly felt sick and frightened. She'd argued with him, but she wasn't that mad. Maybe he'd gotten those stains walking somewhere else in the night after their argument. But suppose everyone jumped to the first thought she'd had, and stayed with it? They might accuse him of being the phantom she'd seen!

"No," she answered a little too loudly. "I don't know anything about the alarm. There was no one by the box when I came out. But . . . but since it's proved to be another false alarm . . . I thought maybe whoever did it had been hiding when I came out so fast. Maybe Uncle Jim had seen him slipping away."

Her uncle shook his head. Constable Rick Tyson and several of the volunteers went to neighboring houses to ask if anyone had seen or heard anything unusual. Some of the firemen went directly home and to bed. Dave Cummins could have too, but he frowned and climbed on Number Two to ride back to the station.

Chief Tyson lingered at the station until the rigs were hooked up to their battery chargers.

"We haven't had a full night's sleep this week. Last week it was arson fires. I'd like to get whoever's back of this."

"It's rough," agreed Joe Hadley. "Bad enough on a regular like me, but worse for the rest of you after a hard day's work at your own businesses."

Tyson pointed to the smears on Dave's coat. "You fall on somebody's lawn getting here?"

Nancy-Jo held her breath. Dave stared at the green stains. But the chief went on before he could answer.

"You learned anything up at college that would help us track down a false-alarm bug? I mean, something we don't already know?"

It was said grudgingly, because the town was proud of its efficient citizen department. But Dave, on this vacation and others, had aroused resentment by declaring there should be a full-time, full-paid department for better efficiency and protection.

6

Some said he had ambitions to become its chief when he finished college.

He fingered his stained coat. "After the prom I staked out on a couple of boxes. I picked the wrong ones," he added wryly. "And I shouldn't have worn a white coat. Come on, Nan. I'll walk you home."

She silently placed her cap on the rack. Thinking of that white phantom, she was glad for the offer of his company. It also worried her. He had something on his mind.

"First," he said, when they were away from the station, "I'm sorry we argued. I'm not apologizing for what I said about you and the rest of the volunteers, but for how I said it."

"It's your right to have beliefs," Nancy-Jo murmured, walking a little closer to him as she eyed the dark shadows ahead. "Dave, do you believe in ghosts?"

"No," he said bluntly. "Why?"

Hoping he wouldn't laugh, she hesitantly told him what she had seen. He shook his head gravely.

"I can't go for it, but I'm glad you told me. This is our first clue to whoever is pulling all these false alarms. It's somebody who wears white, at least he did tonight. Now if we can just—" He became aware that she was staring at his coat. "Nan! You don't think—"

"I don't want to, Dave," she said in a contrite, small voice. "That's why . . . it has to be a ghost."

He stared at her. "The dew on those bushes might make green stains. And I'll bet I'm the only guy in town that has them on a white coat." He suddenly grasped her arm and pointed toward a police car standing near the corner. "Rick Tyson must still be questioning neighbors. We'll tell him what you . . . what we're thinking."

Nancy-Jo held back. "No, Dave. Please. He and his father haven't liked what you've been saying about the volunteers. So don't risk—"

Dave interrupted. "It's too late, Nan. I've stepped on too many toes. Sooner or later they'll kick back. And if you, of all people, couldn't avoid suspecting I might be trying to run the volunteers ragged with false alarms so they'll agree with me—"

"I know you wouldn't stoop to doing it that way, Dave," she insisted.

"Others," he declared, "might not be so open-minded. Suspicion, Nan, is like a smoldering fire. If you don't get it out in the open, you can't lick it."

Before she could argue further, he called to Rick who was moving down the walk toward his car. Nancy-Jo reluctantly told her story. The red-headed constable, son of the fire chief, listened with expressionless face and half-squinted eyes.

"A ghost?" he remarked incredulously. "Why didn't you mention it when my father questioned you? Or didn't you know about a ghost . . . until you cooked it up with Dave?"

He swung his light on Dave. "Don't leave," he snapped, then pointed his light into the bushes. Nancy-Jo and Dave followed him in his search. There were no signs of footprints, no branches or twigs that might have been broken by someone crashing through in flight from the alarm box.

8

"So it was a ghost . . . maybe," Rick commented. He played his light on Dave's green stains. "You've got more of them than before. And they all match."

Dave bristled. Nan shot him an I-told-you-so look, then confronted Rick.

"No maybe about it. A ghost pulled that false alarm. You didn't find Dave's footprints in there. And to clear him further, let's go back to the station and put the cold light on his hands."

She caught her breath. Had she said too much? Suppose the cold light revealed a blue stain on Dave's fingers from the chemical, invisible but telltale, that fire departments have on their alarm boxes? Even wearing gloves to pull a false alarm did not prevent signs of incrimination under a cold light. She gave Dave a frightened look.

"I'm willing," he said. "Let's get that light, Rick."

The constable scowled. "Because you know it won't prove anything about you?" His glance swung to Nancy-Jo. "What about your hands? Maybe you've been pulling boxes to prove to him that the volunteers can respond almost as fast as regulars."

"I have not!" Nancy-Jo cried. She unclenched her hands, held them out palm up. "I'll hold them under that light anytime!"

She kept her shoulder in front of Dave who looked as though he wanted to sock Rick.

"Skip it," Rick muttered. "If we start that, we'll have to do it to the whole department, including my father. We're all getting too tense." He sighed.

"Looks like I've got a ghost to catch," he said dryly, then drove off slowly.

Dave glowered after him, then peered at the dark bushes.

"I can't believe it either . . . but I've got to."

Nancy-Jo shivered. "I wish I weren't the only one who had seen it. I wish . . . I wish I hadn't seen it at all!"

Rick must have spoken to his father, and his father relayed it to customers who came into the hardware store. By noon, rumors, fears and suspicions shimmered like the June heat. People argued pro and con. Ghosts? No such thing! There sure were! Why should a ghost pull false alarms? It wasn't a ghost. It was just a tall tale to divert suspicion from someone who wanted to prove a point. And you know who! And she is helping him cover up his activities!

Nancy-Jo bit her lip when she sensed, and sometimes overheard, those insinuations. She should have insisted that Dave keep her story to himself.

When night came, the streets were strangely deserted, early. Believers in ghosts, and non-believers, carefully closed up the lower floors of their homes despite the warm night. Nancy-Jo couldn't sleep. Too tense, waiting. She shivered by her bedroom window. Watching. Watching. Thinking she saw something, but knowing she didn't.

Wait!

Something did move down there in the deep blackness close to the bushes. It wasn't white this

10

time. Just a darker substance than the shadows. Her trembling fingers closed about a flashlight. It felt like ice in her hand. Did she dare face it? Don't scream now! She aimed the light and pressed the button.

A small white blob whipped around in her direction—Dave's startled face. He came closer under her window.

"I've been watching," he called softly, but didn't say whether he meant the alarm box or thought she needed protection. He shook his head between hunched shoulders as he looked up at her. "Man, when that light suddenly glowed on the bushes around me . . . like a ghost! Is my hair gray?"

Nancy-Jo laughed tensely. "Is mine?" she asked. "Because when I first saw you move . . . wait, I'll come down."

She dressed warmly, but the night felt cold. Dave put his arm around her shoulders reassuringly, but briefly, too briefly.

"Are you mad?" Nancy-Jo asked. "I wouldn't blame you if—"

"I still think the same about volunteers versus regulars," he muttered. "Let's not argue about it. People who don't believe in ghosts are going to make us scapeghosts . . . I mean, scapegoats . . . if we don't clear up these false alarms, these ghost alarms. I've been thinking, why do they always occur at night?"

"That's when ghosts usually operate," Nancy-Jo began.

"But why not in the daytime?" Dave demanded.

11

"From what little I know about ghosts, if there are such things, they usually can't be seen in daylight. So why doesn't our ghost pull an alarm then? He, she, or it, would be perfectly safe. But it's always at night."

Nancy-Jo nodded, fighting the urge to switch on the flashlight and keep it moving about in the darkness.

"Who is it trying to scare? What's it trying to prove?" She bit her lip. "Dave, let's map out all those false alarms."

"Good idea," he agreed. "I'll go down to the station now."

"I'll go too," Nancy-Jo said. "I can't sleep anyway."

She didn't add that it wasn't just a ghost alone that was making her sleepless with worry. She was proud of being a member of the volunteer department which Dave wanted to eliminate. Helping him clear himself of suspicion could mean the loss of her status. But wasn't Dave more important? She linked her arm with his as they went along the dark street.

"We'll get to the bottom of it somehow."

"I've got to," he declared. "How will it look at school, or in the future after graduation, if I've been suspected and accused of pulling false alarms? I've got to clear myself."

The office door of the fire station opened as they approached. Stodgy Mort Garner, the town produce and feed dealer, came out, looking sleepy and mad.

"A fine business," he snapped. "Trying to collect

bills at night because I'm too bushed to keep up with daytimes. You two looking for that ghost? You better find it fast, or else . . ."

Dave nodded grimly and opened the door. Nancy-Jo went in, then gasped at the sight of a mouse on the desk before Joe Hadley.

"He's tame, Nan. Won't harm you." Hadley grinned proudly. "Watch!" He made a signaling motion with his fingers. The mouse rolled over, then sat up to nibble a rewarding crumb of bread.

Nancy-Jo felt something nibbling the back of her neck. It made squeaking sounds. She shrieked and jumped aside, discovering that Dave had been teasing. The mouse on the desk fled from sight. Hadley scowled.

"Now it'll take a couple days to win back his confidence."

"Sorry," Dave murmured. "I want to check the last two weeks of alarms." He pulled open a drawer and spoke absently. "Why did you ever give up the circus anyway?"

"Too much night work." Hadley yawned. "Not that I've been getting solid sleep on this job lately, not since—" He closed his mouth hard and uncomfortably avoided Dave's stare.

"Not since Dave's been home," Nancy-Jo thought. "I'm ready," she told him, and picked up a box of colored pins. As Dave called out locations where there had been false alarms, or night fires that had obviously been set, she marked them on the big map of town. Then she, Dave, and Hadley studied them.

"They're all over town," Hadley muttered. "That ghost sure gets around. I don't see any pattern, do you?"

Dave shook his head disappointedly. Nancy-Jo felt there had to be some message in the setup of those pins. But what? She squinted at the map, in the hope that closing out other details might reveal something.

Hadley shrugged. "I'm going to turn in. When you two leave, just set the spring locks and close the doors. I'll take care of the rear."

Dave continued scowling at the map a long time. "I thought sure we'd spot something."

"What? The ghost?" Nancy-Jo shivered and wished she hadn't reminded herself. "Dave," she suggested, "let's just concentrate on the false alarms. We've got good reason to believe it might have pulled at least one of them, last night. So let's try. I'll get different colored pins."

She searched through the desk, pawing down past mimeographed forms, vouchers for rig equipment, unsold tickets to the last firemen's carnival and local circus talent, some pin-up pictures which Dave wanted to see, but she firmly closed the drawer.

"I'm the pin-up girl tonight," she declared, waving a box of pins.

Dave went to the file again and called out the false alarm locations once more. Nancy-Jo became excited as she exchanged the pins.

"Dave, look!" Green pins, representing false

14

alarms, almost formed a circle around the heart of town. "Could that mean," she asked with a shudder, "the ghost lives inside that circle, right in among us?"

Dave frowned. "Some people would also say that circle is almost centered on where I live."

Nancy-Jo stared. "My home too." Her voice became worried. "I saw the ghost coming from the box . . . but Uncle Jim and Aunt Sue can't prove I didn't do it, that I was in bed when the alarm sounded. I guess that would apply to the other false alarms too, or most of them. They're such heavy sleepers." She grasped Dave's arm. "And what about you?"

"Not much alibi either," he muttered. He pointed at the map. "But I'm going to make that ghost find an alibi, if it can. There are two alarm boxes that haven't been pulled to complete that circle. Nan, I'm going to keep watch on them."

Nancy-Jo hesitated, then tried not to sound scared. "You can't watch both. You take one and . . . and I'll take the other."

"Nothing doing. We don't know what we're up against. You're not going to be out there alone. I'll get Rick Tyson to watch the other box."

Nancy-Jo let him escort her home after he called Rick on the radio and arranged for a meeting. Wishing Dave good luck, she closed and locked the door, but she didn't go upstairs. She stood there, peering through the curtains, watching Dave hurrying away into the darkness. Suppose Rick didn't

co-operate? Then again, being the only night constable on patrol, he might be called away to an
accident or some other police matter. One box
would then be left unwatched.

Nancy-Jo slipped out onto the porch and paused,
trembling, summoning her nerve. Somewhere off
in the night there was a slam like a car door or
trunk lid. She jumped. Just people, she told herself.
Maybe Rick meeting Dave down the street in the
opposite direction from the fire station. She'd better
not let them see her. She went slowly down the
walk, looking in that direction. And then . . .

Moannnnn . . .

It reverberated right through her. The fire horn
again. She whipped around, and there was the white
phantom gliding away from the box on her corner!

She didn't want to, but her muscles, contracting
in sudden fright, forced out a piercing scream. A
car swung out of the next street. The driver didn't
hear her. He went on toward the fire station. And
she had eyes only for that phantom blob vanishing
into the darkness toward the bushes. It had paused
when she'd screamed. Now it bobbed into motion
again . . . and she was running after it! What on
earth possessed her? She might catch it! What
then! She slowed, then realized that the ghost was
afraid of her!

That gave her new angry courage, not much, but
enough to dash after it again, afraid it would get
away, afraid it wouldn't. In the blackness it rose
up like a white wraith and streamed through the

16

bushes. She heard leaves rustling, the swish of branches. She crashed in pursuit, but the bushes had bony arms and clawing fingers that restrained her. The ghost vanished ahead, getting away.

And that fire horn kept moaning, moaning, moaning . . .

Nancy-Jo heard feet running along the street toward the fire station. She called loudly.

"Never mind the rigs! Go around the block! Head it off, it's getting away!"

She heard men shout to each other. Someone pointed a flashlight at her.

"It's Nancy-Jo!"

By the time she made them understand she wanted them to go around the block—to head off a ghost—she knew it was too late. One man stood in the street, waving a flashlight and shouting to volunteers converging up at the fire station. Cars came right on down ahead of Number One Rig. There were brief consultations. Some of them shot away around the block.

Then a crowd gathered around Nancy-Jo as she gasped and sobbed with reaction. Excited voices ringed her. Then she saw Chief Tyson, his son, Rick, and Dave. They frowned.

The chief said, "No one's seen any sign of . . . of a ghost, Nancy-Jo."

"But I did," she exclaimed, breathlessly. "And I'm beginning to think I have an idea—"

"I'm sorry," the chief said. "I don't like to do this, but I've got to, for your own protection."

17

He thumbed the switch of the big cold light. Nancy-Jo heard gasps and muttered comments from the volunteers and onlookers. Glancing down, she sucked her breath as she saw a glowing, bluish smear on her right palm. The telltale, incriminating chemical from an alarm box. There was another smudgy glow on her sleeve. Another on her blouse.

Someone's voice rose with suspicious accusation. "She ought to know that trying to rub or wash it off makes it worse."

Nancy-Jo shook her head. "But I didn't—"

"Never mind an alibi," sour-faced Mort Garner snapped. "We can see the evidence. It's not a ghost that only you can see."

"Give her a chance," Dave demanded, and was shouted down.

Nancy-Jo stared at the smear across her shaking palm. Then she faced the chief.

"If . . . if I pulled that false alarm . . ."

"No ifs," Mort Garner began. Dave grabbed him. The chief pulled him back and barked for everyone to be silent.

"All right, Nan," he said resignedly. "What is it?"

Nancy-Jo had a ghost of a thought, but knew that before anyone would listen to it she would first have to clear herself, if she could.

"Chief," she asked slowly, holding out her stained hand, "how many people can get a palm into the narrow opening of an alarm box, at least those we have in this town? If I pulled that box, wouldn't I have the stain on my fingers?"

18

A voice jeered. "She's just hairsplitting." Others joined in. How could she explain the chemical on her hands if she hadn't been near the box as she claimed? Nancy-Jo raised her voice.

"I chased the ghost. I must have touched bushes it had touched, and I must have brushed against others."

"Oh, the ghost again! If a ghost can go through walls as though they're not there, why should a chemical stick to it?"

Nancy-Jo held the chief's troubled gaze. "Please . . . will you point your light at the bushes?"

Rick Tyson shook his head pityingly. Big Sam Tyson sighed, then moved closer to the bushes and thumbed the light switch.

Like jewels in the dark velvet of night, a strung-out necklace of blue glows appeared on branches. They were bright close at hand. Those farther back were dim, but brightened as the astonished chief advanced with the light.

Dave shouted. "That's proof she's not making it up about a ghost!"

People crowded around her. What did the ghost look like? Others wanted to borrow the chief's light and follow the trail. Chief Tyson pushed them away.

"You said you had an idea, Nan," he prompted.

Nancy-Jo almost wished she hadn't mentioned it as she stood, surrounded by intent faces. Mort Garner stared at her. Joe Hadley peered down from the rig. Dave watched her hopefully. She had to go through with it. And she'd better be right, because she knew how it felt to be wrongly accused. She turned abruptly to Mort Garner.

"What were you doing at the fire station tonight?"

He paled as all eyes turned toward him. "I-I told you. I was trying to collect . . . a bill."

"From whom? What kind of a bill?" Nancy-Jo asked.

Garner jerked his arm toward Joe Hadley. "From him. For those animals he keeps from his circus days. They take a lot of feed. But what's that got to do with—"

The crowd melted back as Nancy-Jo moved closer to Number One rig.

"What kind of animals are they, Joe?"

"You've seen my back-yard zoo," he declared. "I had it at the last firemen's carnival and circus. A couple of dogs, a pony, small bear, mice. Everybody's seen them when they've brought their pets out for me to train."

Nancy-Jo looked up at him. "Why don't you mention the monkeys, Joe?"

"Sure," he snapped. "I got some. Everybody knows that too." He smiled grimly. "They're black and brown. Rhesus monks."

"I've been to other zoos," Nancy-Jo said quietly. "I've seen white, or are they gray, spider monkeys. One of those would be just about the right size for the supposed ghost I've seen here the past two nights."

"You're nuts!" he barked.

Someone called from back in the crowd. "A gray monkey swinging through bushes in the dark would look as though it was drifting through. It would leave chemical stains too if its paw had just pulled the box." Others shouted. "Let's go out to your place, Joe, and have a look around." Then a louder voice. "Hey, here's a bit of gray or white fur caught on a branch."

Nancy-Jo saw Hadley's eyes widen. He suddenly meshed the rig's gears. She scrambled up, reaching for the ignition key. Dave lunged past her and grabbed Hadley.

"I get it now," Dave accused. "You took advantage of what I've been saying about a regular department. You saw a chance to force a full-time better-paying job by running the volunteers ragged with night alarms. Last week, when you weren't on night duty, you set fires. This week, you had a spider monkey trained to pull boxes."

"I live two miles out of town," Hadley retorted. "If I left the station to drive way out there and back—"

"You didn't have to go home," Nancy-Jo interrupted. "Someone look at his car back of the station." She remembered what she'd heard and seen when she'd come out of the house just before the alarm sounded tonight. "He's probably got a cage in the trunk. Late at night he drove just a few blocks from the station, released the monkey near an alarm box, then raced back to be here before the alarm sounded."

Rick Tyson confronted Hadley. "It's all fitting together, and you *know* it will. So . . ."

"All right," Hadley muttered. He'd built an alarm box and trained the monkey to pull the box before it would be fed. He also taught it how to find its way home. When it pulled a false alarm it knew there would be a meal waiting for it in the pen at home.

When he'd seen the pins Nancy-Jo put on the map, he knew she and Dave were getting too close. He surmised they were going to watch two boxes, so he released the monkey to pull this one on the corner again because it wouldn't be watched.

Rick Tyson placed him under arrest. Chief Tyson shook his head as he spoke to Hadley.

"You needn't have tried to force things to prove Dave was right about a department of regulars. The underwriters have been telling me the town's getting too big to depend on volunteers." He sighed. "Guess I'll be out of this job soon."

"And so will I," Nancy-Jo murmured as she and Dave stood on the porch after the others had gone.

Dave put his arm around her, and this time kept it there.

"It had to happen sooner or later, Nan. It always does when towns grow, and people grow with them. Everyone's just got to be ready to . . . to take on new ways of life." He looked down at her. "When I finish college, I hope it won't be too long before I can offer you a new, lifetime career."

Nancy-Jo smiled up at him.

"Do you think you'd have a . . . a ghost of a chance?"

But she already knew the answer, and let him know, silently, when his lips came down to hers.

Ghost of Black John

―◆――◆――◆――◆―

WILLIAM MAC KELLAR

A SOFT mist drifted down from the mountains wreathing the trees in drab gray mantles so that they stood out in the gloomy half light like dispirited and abandoned ghosts. Wearily Chuck Adams withdrew his face from the window.

"Rain and fog and herring! I wonder if the sun ever shines in these Scottish islands? Boy, will I be glad to see Long Island again!"

Mrs. Adams smiled over at her son.

"It's really not that bad, Chuck. At least the people in the Hebrides who live here all the year round don't mind it. Besides we'll only be here for a few more weeks until your father finishes his survey for the government."

"Just the same, Pop can't finish counting these herring soon enough for me. No kidding, did you ever see such a sleepy place?"

"It's quiet, naturally, Chuck. And it's not just counting herring. Your father has been invited by

25

the British Government to suggest methods of processing and canning herring. It will mean more fish for the people in Scotland."

"They can have my share," he said, "anytime!" He went over to the window and gazed disconsolately at the desolate scene that met his eye. The mist had lifted somewhat and gray, ominous clouds scudded past, trailing thin serpents of vapor over the bleak mountain tops. What a place!

Suddenly he spied the compact figure of a boy coming towards the cottage from the direction of the glen. Chuck turned to his mother with a smile.

"Here comes Sandy MacLean with the weekly newspaper! Beats me how they ever get enough news to fill it." He opened the door and greeted the dark haired youth.

"A *bonnie* day, is it no?" Sandy's voice rose and fell in the gentle Highland tongue. His speech held little of the difficult brogue that the American boy had assumed was natural to all Scotsmen.

"A *bonnie* day?" repeated Chuck, startled. "Why it's raining!"

The ghost of a smile visited the Scottish boy's lips. *"Och,* but the sun will be out soon, Chuck. Wind, sun, and rain; it's lucky we are in the islands to see so much of nature."

What's the sense of arguing, thought Chuck. He wouldn't understand. Besides he's really not a bad fellow. A little serious in his ways but friendly enough. Glancing at him covertly again, Chuck marked the finely developed shoulders under the heavy wool jersey and the strong, thick fingers that cupped the newspapers. Make a good end back home, he thought.

"Anything new, Sandy?" said Chuck glancing hopefully at the front page of the paper. "Surely something must happen here once in a while?"

"Well, now, there will be the new minister coming soon," intoned Sandy in his soft voice, *"aye* something it seems."

Chuck nodded wearily and tossed the paper over on the bureau. "I can imagine," he muttered absently. He was instantly aware the Scottish boy was eyeing him quietly. "No offense Sandy. It's just that, well, a tiny island off the Scottish coast. I mean, what should I expect to happen here?" He hoped he hadn't offended him.

A tiny glint of light glimmered in the brooding eyes of the Scottish youth. "There will be things happening this day on the island," he said softly, "that in all America there will not be the like."

"What things?" said Chuck.

"Oh, things," repeated Sandy slyly. "Like ghosts for instance."

"Ghosts?" echoed Chuck sharply. Had he heard right?

The Scottish boy nodded, and his furtive, mysterious manner gave way to an expression of quiet, Gaelic pride.

"Aye, for there's few places indeed can boast of a ghost the like of Black John."

"You're not telling me that you believe in ghosts?" Chuck could hardly control his amazement.

"It was three hundred years ago that Black John,

he that in the Gaelic tongue is called *Iain Dubh,* saw his son leave for the sea. He never returned. But the old man would not believe he was dead. *Aye,* every penny he had he spent in the search for him. And when he died, poor and lonely, he was no less faithful. For the ghost of him continued to wait by the water, wrapped in the shrouds of his burial and with a lantern to guide his son home."

He stopped and a look of stubborn pride burned deep in his eyes. "I myself have seen him."

Chuck felt his jaw slacken in astonishment as Sandy recited the story.

"You believe in ghosts?" was all he could say.

"In the ghost of Black John, *aye,*" answered Sandy.

It's too crazy to continue talking about, thought Chuck. He stuck his hands deep in his pockets, whistled lightly, and sauntered over to the window.

"You will be thinking Black John does not exist, Chuck?" The soft cadence of the Highland boy's tongue held no note of resentment or annoyance. Only the dark eyes, recessed behind the heavy brows, glowed.

Chuck shrugged with good-humored indifference. Before he could answer, the door opened and his father's friendly voice rang out in the kitchen.

"Boy, am I tired! Really cold out in the water this morning." As he drew off his sea boots his eyes fell on the Scottish boy. "Hello, Sandy! Stay with us for lunch?"

"Thank you, Mr. Adams, but it's myself should be getting along with my papers, I'm thinking." He paused at the door. "There will be those anxious for the news. Good day!"

As the door closed softly behind him Chuck scratched his head in bewilderment. "Imagine anyone believing in ghosts today? I didn't mean to offend Sandy but this business of Black John!" He shook his head in baffled resignation.

"Black John?" repeated Chuck's father with a frown. "I've been hearing about him. Something of a local celebrity, I guess. Talking about celebrities, we had a few government inspectors from Glasgow today. Seems there's quite a bit of smuggling lately."

"Sure wish somebody would smuggle some of those herring out of here," muttered Chuck gloomily as he eyed his mother's preparations for lunch. "If I eat any more they'll be putting a label on me and shipping me back to America in a can," he said with mock horror.

Some time later that day he again met Sandy. The latter was apparently headed for the *clachan,* or small village, where he lived, but he paused when he saw Chuck.

"Perhaps, Chuck, you would be liking to see Black John for yourself?"

Chuck stared at him. It was about time he settled this business once and for all. "Listen, Sandy," he said bluntly. "I don't want to hurt your feelings, but frankly I wish you'd stop all this talk about ghosts."

"But it's myself has seen him walking from the ruined castle on the mountain of Ben-y-Gloe to the sea." Sandy paused and the quiet intensity left him

29

to be replaced by an expression of amused, indulgent challenge. "Perhaps being a stranger you would be a wee bit reluctant to see for yourself."

Chuck felt a hot flush of anger charge through him.

"Afraid of an old wives' tale?" he scoffed. "Anytime you plan a visit to your pet ghost, Sandy, let me know."

Sandy nodded. "Tonight then?" and the same mocking smile was on his lips as he softly said goodbye.

"Tonight," said Chuck grimly. He watched the Scottish lad as he made his way with long, easy strides to his cottage. It would give him a lot of pleasure to convince Sandy that there were no more ghosts in the Hebrides than there were in Babylon, Long Island.

The heavy mists from the sea had rolled away and the night was clear and cool as the boys made their way silently across the field of heather and bracken towards the grim bulk of Ben-y-Gloe, the Mountain of the Mist. A yellow moon, knee-deep in little pools of gossamer clouds sifted a soft light over the stark scene and illuminated the sheer precipice that swept down to the sea. Far off, Chuck could hear the low boom of the Atlantic breakers as they dashed against the rocks. He shivered.

"You're sure old John will be home tonight, Sandy?" He tried to make his voice sound casual, but deep inside he could feel his heart press against his ribs in measured throbs of excitement.

"Perhaps. We shall see."

The Scottish boy said no more and for the next half hour Chuck followed him in silence as they clambered up the narrow trail that ran perilously along the black cliff. Once Chuck's eyes strayed to the great abyss that yawned up just a foot from the path. A clammy shiver of fear gripped him and his head swam before he desperately swept his eyes back to the trail. Quite suddenly he felt the ground beneath him level off. They were at the top of Ben-y-Gloe.

Soundlessly Sandy pulled him down and pointed. Chuck stared in unbelief at the sight that met his eyes.

Silhouetted in stark relief against the moon, a huge black mass of rock soared up from the earth a mere hundred yards away. What must once have been among the noblest Hebridean castles was now a forlorn heap of weather-beaten, ivy-strewed boulders; but three of its enormous walls stood in some semblance of preservation, and one of its four original turrets continued to face the sea. Something about the melancholy ruin, something menacing and evil, caused tiny beads of perspiration to gather on Chuck's forehead despite the sharp chill in the air.

"The house of Black John," came Sandy's voice, brittle with tenseness. Again Chuck struggled to repel the nameless aura of dread that sifted out from the gloomy castle. Again he shivered.

Silently they inched their way on their stomachs across the sparsely vegetated ground towards the grim pile of crumbling stone from whence, three-hundred years ago, Black John had seen his son depart for the sea. Suddenly from the turret of the castle came a quick stab of light. It was gone as quickly as it had come.

"Did you see that?" The words seemed to pry themselves out from between Chuck's clenched teeth.

Sandy nodded. "It is Black John lighting his lantern," he whispered and Chuck felt his skin crawl in a horror he had never known in all his life.

Again there was a flash of light, only now the light came not from the tower but from an aperture in the wall facing the sea.

"He is coming down to look for his son," said Sandy gripping Chuck's arm.

Chuck nodded, afraid that the excitement in his voice might betray him.

"Here he comes!" Sandy's voice was a low hiss beside him. Again Chuck nodded and crouched lower behind a tussock of heather as the flickering light moved slowly away from the castle towards where they lay concealed. Slowly, as the seconds passed, it became possible to discern the outlines of a gaunt, shapeless figure. A figure wrapped in a long, black, funeral shroud. The ghost of Black John.

Chuck's breath froze in his throat as the long dead Highland chieftain made his way slowly towards the sea that had taken his son three centuries ago. He passed only a few feet from where the boys lay, the lantern held rigidly in a bony hand.

"Let us go," whispered Sandy after the spectre had passed. "It is bad luck to watch a man's sorrow." He paused. "Listen."

Slowly at first and then in ever-rising tremolos of despair a bloodless wail floated from the lips of the gaunt figure on the edge of the cliff.

"It is Black John calling to his dead son," said Sandy in a low voice, "It is bad luck. Let us go."

"One minute, Sandy." Despite his fear and dread Chuck lingered. There had been something a moment ago that only now made him pause. Something just as the ghost of Black John passed them. A tiny glint of clear blue light on one of the scrawny fingers that clutched the lantern.

"If Black John spent all his wealth looking for his son, Sandy, why is he wearing a diamond on his finger?"

"A diamond?" repeated Sandy. He stopped as the American youth dug his fingers sharply into his arm and pointed.

"Look, Sandy, he's signaling to someone out in the water!" Transfixed with wonder the boys watched as the light blinked in spaced intervals of lights and dark. Then holding their breaths, impelled by an urgency to discover more, they pulled themselves carefully along on their stomachs towards the cliff edge. A scant ten yeards away the hooded figure of Black John continued the systematic flashings of his lantern.

Slowly the minutes passed as the boys gazed, fascinated, at the weird spectacle being enacted before them. At regular intervals an eerie wail would break from Black John's lips, and each time Chuck could feel his blood run cold within him. And then quite suddenly there was a scrape of a shoe and a voice called cautiously up from below.

"Charlie?"

"Who else?" barked the lantern waver, and Chuck jumped as he heard the shrouded figure speak. "You've got the stuff, Dave?"

The other grunted affirmatively and pulled himself up over the edge of the cliff. "I'll be right glad when this business is finished," he panted. "Secret trail or not, it's no fun climbing up that cliff at night."

"Shut up, will you?" snapped Charlie, alias Black John. "I'm taking the real risk. What if those local half-wits found out who I am?"

Chuck stared in horror at Sandy. It was easy to see now who was at the bottom of this smuggling business!

"It's the last haul," the man called Charlie was speaking. "We're pulling out tonight. What was that?"

Chuck froze. In seeking to ease his cramped position, his foot had dislodged a small stone. He listened, numb with dread, as it clattered down the precipice.

"I don't know but I'll find out," growled the other advancing on the boys. A slender blade flashed in his hand.

There was just one thing to do, and the boys did it. Before the astonished Dave was aware of their presence, Chuck lunged desperately and grabbed him tightly around the ankles. At the same moment Sandy, running low, hurled himself viciously at the smuggler's mid-section. With a grunt of pain and surprise, the man toppled over on the heather as the boys dashed wildly past the infuriated Charlie encased in his long shroud.

"Make for the castle," cried Chuck knowing full well that they could never hope to surprise the smugglers a second time in any free-for-all. Sandy nodded and tucking his head down low fairly skimmed over the ground towards the castle with the two men thundering behind.

The boys reached the castle simultaneously and immediately darted into the shadows. "In here," whispered Chuck, as he pulled himself up to an opening in the massive wall. With a quick effort Sandy gripped the ledge firmly and scrambled up with the American youth.

Carefully they let themselves down into the darkness on the other side. A damp, musty smell assailed Chuck's nostrils and he extended his hand gingerly before him. Something cold brushed against his fingers. He drew himself back sharply before he realized what he had touched. Iron chains. They were in the dungeon of the castle!

"I saw them! This way!" a voice cried out from above them, and with a single action Chuck and Sandy stumbled across the room hoping to find nearby an exit to the outside.

Suddenly Chuck's fingers, urgently groping along the moist rock wall of the dungeon, came in contact with a horizontal beam of wood. The cross-bar of a door! With a quick heave he raised it and, swinging the ancient door wide, dashed frantically up the spiral stairs with Sandy by his side.

It wasn't until they reached the uppermost portion of the castle that Chuck realized they were trapped. There was no way out except the way they had just come up!

Chuck looked around desperately. He could hear the pounding of the smugglers' shoes on the ancient stairs. Wildly he looked around for something with which to defend themselves and his heart sank as he saw the barrenness of the small tower into which they had been chased.

"Quick, Chuck, the ivy!" It was Sandy calling as he scrambled over the parapet.

Like an agile monkey Chuck slithered over the wall after his friend. His fingers wound fiercely around the hardy growth that enveloped that portion of the castle and, releasing one hand after the other he followed Sandy closely down the wall. Once a clump of ivy came away sickeningly in his hand and only a quick lunge by Sandy held him until he could get a fresh grip.

"The door to the stairs!" panted Chuck frantically as they reached the ground, "hurry, before they get there!"

There wasn't a moment to spare. Already the smugglers, realizing that the ivy could not bear their greater weight, were clattering furiously down the long stairway they had just ascended. Racing around the wall the boys made for the dungeon opening. As they scrambled through the narrow embrasure they practically hurled themselves into the inky blackness of the dungeon.

"Over there," panted Chuck, directed by the clatter of the approaching men. The ring of their boots on the stone steps resounded in the dungeon with terrifying violence. The smugglers could have been no more than three steps away when Sandy's straining hands brushed against the door. It was the work of a second to slam it tight as Chuck brought down the crossbar. A baffled roar came from the other side as the two smugglers pounded on the barred door.

Without lingering further, Sandy and Chuck scrambled out of the dungeon and ran as swiftly as their remaining strength allowed away from the castle. Crashing wildly down the trail, they finally reached the glen at the bottom of the fearsome Ben-y-Gloe. From there it was only a short journey across the bogs to Chuck's house where they blurted out their story to an anxious Mr. and Mrs. Adams.

"Smugglers!" snapped Chuck's father after he had assured himself that the boys were all right. "We'll take care of that. You two wait here while I get the police and go after them!"

It was some time later that Chuck's father and the local constables returned. In their midst were the two smugglers, manacled together and looking decidedly unhappy about the whole thing. The one called Charlie, still in his long black shroud, cast a baleful glance at the boys as he passed with the police on his way to the jail.

Chuck couldn't suppress a grin. "Now there's a fellow who is really dressed up for his own funeral," he chuckled.

"*Aye*," added Sandy drily, "and with his own ghost, no less, to haunt him." He paused and directed a rueful smile at Chuck. "Talking of ghosts, I've been a wee bit of a fool I'm thinking."

"No more than I've been, Sandy." Chuck colored slightly. He turned impulsively to the Scottish boy and thrust out his hand. Sandy's firm grip was friendliness itself.

There was little sleep in the village that night. Everyone wanted to hear the boys' story and to congratulate them on breaking up the smuggling ring.

"It was really quite clever," said Chuck's father after the boys had finished for the tenth time their account of the night's happenings. "These two smugglers knew that the local people here have a genuine respect for ghosts. What could be simpler than to play the role of old Black John? The flashing lights and the ghostly wailings would be sure to keep folks away while at the same time our two friends unloaded their illegal merchandise." Mr. Adams nodded his head in approval. "Yes, very clever, indeed—almost professional."

"But how did they get the stuff off this island to the mainland?" said Chuck curiously. "That's what beats me. They must have been slick."

His father crimsoned slightly. "Seems they were

smuggling it out with my herring," he said, casting a sheepish glance at his wife, while the two boys burst into convulsions of laughter.

"You know, Sandy," said Chuck as he showed the Scottish boy to the door, "I take back everything I said about nothing's ever happening in the Hebrides. I've had enough excitement tonight to last me a year."

Sandy smiled, "Then you will be back next year, Chuck? Aye, we could have a *bonnie* time of it."

"I sure will," said Chuck with a wide grin, "even if I've got to come back as a herring to do it."

Dark Flowers

KAY HAUGAARD

THE rubes were being herded into the dark opening one by one. Clad in their shapelss overalls and huge black galoshes, they resembled a herd of silent grey elephants.

Greta Lindgren waited impatiently for her friend Dick Thomas to guide the last ponderously garbed tourist through the uninviting opening before she started down the steep metal steps into the cave. Entering from the golden sunshine of the summer day it seemed darker, even damper, with a chill that clung like a clammy blanket.

"Watch your step ladies and gentlemen. I will not deceive you into thinking the caves are entirely safe. The ladders are slippery and so are the paths."

Dick reached up and took the hand of a woman whose grey hair was frizzed into little knots. She was clutching her enormous, flower-covered straw purse incongruently against her tarpaulin-like overalls. She appeared frightened.

41

"As long as you do not stray from the regular path and watch your step carefully, there is nothing one by one. Clad in their shapeless overalls and ing to fear, ma'am." Dick brought the woman safely down from the ladder onto the damp dirt path beside him.

Greta ducked her head automatically to avoid a low hanging stalactite. She had followed Dick through on these tours so many times during her time off from her job at the gift shop that she practically knew his spiel by heart. Her first trip through at the beginning of June, when she had just arrived to work for the summer, had awed and terrified her. Now she felt she could grope her way under the stalactites and between the stalagmites (stalactites stick "tite" to the ceiling, stalagmites "mite" if they could, she remembered, feeling immensely clever that she had) between the pillars, down the ladders, up the ladders, over the "Frozen Lake," through the "Great Hall," down the "Catacomb Corridor" and out into the daylight without even the assistance of a flashlight.

The group of tourists walked down the narrow dirt path that edged a deep chasm filled with an angry, jagged mass of rock made menacingly alive by the shifting fingers of shadow caused by Dick's swinging lantern.

"On your left, ladies and gentlemen, you will see, 'Dante's Inferno.' It has been so named because of its imagined similarity to the 'Pit.' If you look closely you will see the glow of the fires." Dick flicked a switch with his boot and the whole bottom of the cavern lit up with a red glow of varied intensity from a hot, searing red in the open light to warm blacks, deepened, and reddened to blood color in the shadows.

There were ooh's and aah's from the tourists. Dick continued with his speech, catching sight of Greta and winking at her openly now that all other heads were directed toward the chasm. "Of course, ladies and gentlemen, this bit of fantasy is a miracle of modern science and one with which we are all familiar. But there is a story about the caves which does not have such a simple explanation. It concerns a young girl named Augusta Guthrie who with her family was passing through this country during the early 1870's in a wagon train."

Then Dick retold the tale Greta knew so well. She had heard it so often that as she leaned against the jagged wall, her arms crossed tightly against the cold, she was not sure whether she was really hearing Dick's voice or hearing her memory of it.

"She wandered off into the woods by herself. The members of the wagon train were able to follow her footsteps to the mouth of the caves, and they searched throughout the portions of the cave they could reach but with no success. She was never found. She is known as the discoverer of the caves. Some say that she is a jealous owner who has not entirely relinquished her treasure even in death. Many persons whose integrity is respected, have sworn they have seen her walking through the higher chambers of the caves; her long calico skirt and sunbonnet ribbons floating in the windless, lightless cave. To some she merelely beckons. Others she approaches and asks plaintively, 'Will they yet return?' and lays a bony hand on them in pleading."

Greta smiled a little and looked down at her oxfords, crossed as she leaned against the cave wall. She felt slightly superior to these open-mouthed creatures staring so eagerly and swallowing so gullibly. Perhaps they would not believe in the sunshine either. They would laugh when they returned to the coffee shop. But now the air seemed heavier, thicker, wet with silent apprehension. Then a man broke in with a nervous laugh.

"Pretty good story, son." He turned to the others. "They just have to throw in a little show for the money, don't they?"

The others laughed with relief.

Greta looked up to Dick for what she knew he would say. He was a wonderful showman. He rose a little above them on the trail ahead and spoke. His voice gathered small enlarging echoes from the huge cave. "The gentleman is right," he said solemnly, "It is wrong to think of this story too seriously. I try not to think of it as I walk the caves alone. Let's go on to other, more pleasant aspects."

Greta thought maybe she wouldn't walk the whole fifty steps up the steel ladder to the "Cathedral," as one small side chamber off the Great Hall was called because of the massive formations which had grown together into groups of towering, translucent pillars resembling a massive pipe organ. She stood at the bottom of the steps as the others walked up slowly. Then, when she was the only one down below, Dick called down the ladder. "Young lady, please do not become separated from the group. I would not be responsible for your safety."

Greta smiled at him and his little game and at the amused titter that spread among the tourists. He wasn't fooling anyone. So she went up and stood packed in the tiny room with the others and listened to his speech while the green lights placed behind the translucent pillars lit the whole thing up like a huge juke box. The green color gave it an eerie quality. Then, as Dick flicked the switch, a flood of music came from the concealed record player. *I Know a Green Cathedral.*

This had always bothered Greta so she used it to kibitz a bit. "But guide, the green cathedral in the song is a forest."

Dick loosed one of his imperturbable grins. "Speak to the management, young lady. I only work here."

Another amused and knowing titter.

At last they had gone through the great hall and turned out all the lights to see what absolute, total and complete darkness really is or how Jonah must have felt under similar circumstances. There was the ritual of lighting the single match and seeing the huge vault of the cavern come alive with warmth and light and the enormously elongated, writhing shadows of people.

Then over the Frozen Lake, down the Catacomb Corridor and home again, home again, jiggety jig. Greta was glad because she was tired of stamping her feet and blowing on her hands to keep warm.

Dick came up to her and took her by the arm. "Hey, rube, let's go get rid of this lamp of mine and we'll see what's for lunch down in ye olde mess hall."

As they climbed the steep hill up from the mess hall after lunch the sun touched them. It filled Greta with a happiness that wanted to express itself.

"Let's climb up to the meadows and see if we can see any deer!"

"Can't. I'm going spelunking tomorrow morning." Dick shoved his hands into his pockets. There was a thoughtful look on his face. It was almost a frown.

"Again!" Greta sighed. "You'd think you'd get enough of that cold, dark old hole." She was disappointed and made no attempt to conceal the fact. "You might get lost in there. You can't go alone."

"Who says I can't? I do all the time. Besides, I know that cave like the face that stares at me from the mirror." He hesitated a bit. "Anyway, I have an idea and I have to prove it."

"Well, I don't care what you say. You might get lost. I'm going with you."

"Oh, it's better, if two of us get lost? No, you can't come. You would get lost on a vacant lot. Besides you'd die of fright if we met up with Ghostly Gussie."

"Oh, you can't scare me out with that ridiculous talk about ghosts. I know you don't believe it any more than I do."

46

Dick looked at her with mock solemnity and shook his head slowly. "Don't be so sure what I believe. I know the caves a little better than you do."

"All right, guide, you can cut the dramatics. I'm no rube, you know. The play is over. I'll meet you in front of the caves at five tomorrow morning."

"I don't believe you will be able to get out of your bed at that hour, but if you do, wear something warmer than a sweater and slacks. Something like long johns and combat boots and an arctic parka. O.K.? We'll be going off the beaten track and baby it's c-c-old down there."

When a quarter to five came next morning, Greta rolled over to turn off her alarm clock to a chorus of groans on the sleeping porch. As she sank back into the soft bed her resolve softened too, then, just as her mind began to blot out reality, she forced herself awake with a jerk, remembering Dick's reproachful words. She staggered out of bed and quickly pulled on her clothes, shivering in the cold, dark morning.

Now she was sitting at the side of the big opening to "The Hole." She was wearing her long red ski underwear, jeans, stadium boots and a couple of woolen shirts over a sweater, and she was wondering vaguely if she could even maneuver in all her gear.

The moon had not yet set and she could see the shape of the hill where the boys' dorm sat, sharply silhouetted against a grey sky. The entire resort area was quiet. There was a lonely moan of breezes in the fir trees. Just the night for a ghost, Greta thought, teasing herself. Aren't they supposed to have a particular fondness for moonlit nights? Well, they aren't any different from their living counterparts in that respect.

Then she looked up and saw a dark shape moving down the path from the boys' bunk house. There was Dick now, she thought, and she got up and started toward him. She had just taken a few steps when a voice behind her startled her.

"I can't believe you got here first. Women are supposed to always be late."

She whirled around to see Dick. He had come from around the hill. "I was getting a flash from the supply house."

"But I . . ." Greta looked up the path to the bunk house but the dark, moving shape was gone. "I thought I saw you coming down the trail from the bunk house just a minute ago."

"Hey girl, get a hold of yourself. We aren't even in the caves and you are seeing things. Are you certain you want to go? We might meet Gussie, you know." His eyes were wide.

The caves were different without the tourists. It did not seem like a big show. It was real. Their footsteps down the metal railing were amplified into huge, hollow echoes by the sounding board of the cave walls.

"We'll go down as far as the Great Hall then I'll check out my idea."

48

Greta did not feel so independent with just the two of them as she had that afternoon with the whole crowd. She stayed close to Dick and the circle of light from the flash that swung and bobbed and reached across the ragged floor.

"Stay here with the flashlight, will you, Greta? I'm going up on that ledge and behind that screen of columns. I've got a hunch I might find something. Just point the flash up the wall; I'll need both hands to climb."

Greta sat down on the damp ledge protruding from the wall and followed Dick's climbing form up the wall with a halo of light. After he got above the loose earth of the lower bank he took a couple of wide-stretched steps up the rocky wall, then he had disappeared behind a curtain of icicle-like pillars. As soon as he disappeared Greta felt alone. It wasn't that she was afraid. Ghosts! Hah! Foolishness!

But it was cold, frightfully cold, and the chill was coming up from the floor and out from the walls. She stamped her feet. She glanced around the huge chamber. There on the wall across from where Dick had gone was a black, amorphous shape that flowed sinuously along the uneven surface, seeming to be coming toward her. Greta gasped. The shapeless appendages were reaching . . . reaching . . . toward her. Her heart strove desperately to break through the cage of her ribs, but she made no sound. She could not scream.

"Found it. Let's go, Miss Persistent." Dick came

bounding down the bank. Greta looked up at Dick with relief, then searched the opposite wall, expecting to see the explanation of the moving shape in his shadow. But Dick's shadow was lying small and docile on the floor. With the light shining toward him his shadow would have to be behind him, not on the opposite wall.

"Come on, I'll show you something you've never seen before." Dick's buoyant cheerfulness made Greta feel better. She pushed the specter or whatever it was to the back of her mind as well as she could. But even as she heard Dick's enthusiastic voice, the thing hovered in her subconscious and she became more and more tense.

Getting down on their hands and knees they wriggled into the opening that Dick had located behind the pillars. Greta followed behind Dick as she pulled herself along on her stomach under the hanging knobs of limestone formations. The floor was wet and muddy. Greta pushed and squirmed toward Dick and his light. Then suddenly the passageway opened wide and there was a fantastically beautiful, high-ceilinged chamber before them.

"Look! We discovered it ourselves! It isn't shown on any map of the caves." Dick was jubilant.

The cavern seemed to be filled with an exotic garden of limestone formations growing lushly from floor and ceiling. Some were fluted and ridged elaborately. Some were bulbous. Some were streaked red from the iron in the limestone, like blood-stained mushrooms. There were golden yellow columns that shaded and faded into smooth, translucent white, reflecting the light damply, glossily.

Greta stared in dumb admiration, not knowing how to express the overwhelming awe flooding in her. It was like finding a globe of crystallized eternity. Everything was so untouched, so pure; a secret treasure deposited by the ages. Time did not seem to exist in this motionless place. Then a drop of cold water fell on Greta's head. She looked up to see another drop swelling on a low-hanging orange stalactite, reminding her that time and motion had penetrated even here.

"Dick! It's the loveliest chamber in the caves. Don't tell anyone about it."

"Kind of reminds me of something I read about the dark flowers that bloom in the mysterious caverns of the soul."

Greta looked at Dick in surprise. She hadn't thought him capable of saying something like that.

"Let's not tell anyone about it, Dick. It would be ruined if we turned it over to the Rubes. There'd be bubble gum stuck all over the formations and 'Joe was here' scratched in the walls." Greta turned to Dick, feeling suddenly earnest and intense, just in time to see his face fading into blackness. The light of the flashlight grew weaker, then brighter, then waved until she could see the white incandescence of the filament outlined by its blue halo. It flared once more before her horrified eyes then died into blackness.

"Dick! What happened, what happened?"

"I . . . don't know. Maybe the batteries. I've

51

been using this flash quite a while. What a dopey thing not to bring batteries . . ."

Greta shivered. The beautiful world of a minute ago had been blotted out completely. She couldn't help thinking of the shadow in the Great Hall and as she shuddered the whole cavern seemed filled with the same, all-devouring shadow swathing them in its dark cloak. She wanted to tell Dick about the shadow but by forming the words it would make it more real so in her subconscious the ghost of Augusta Guthrie grew ever larger, more palpable. She strove to keep it from being conscious. As long as Dick was not afraid, she could borrow from his strength. "What'll we do, Dick? Can we feel our way back?"

"We'd better be able to, we're so far back now no one would ever hear us yell. Greta, here, hold my hand. We can't get separated in here, we'd be sunk, . . . Hey! I've got a couple of matches."

Dick struck one of the matches and illumined the chamber. They looked around for their entrance. The formations had a strange sameness. They were too unfamiliar. There were no landmarks they could use. Dick struck another match when the first had burned his fingers. Then, in the light of the third match, they saw an opening.

"Come on." Dick was feeling his way toward the opening. "If we can get to the Great Hall, I know where there's a supply of batteries near the steps up to the Cathedral."

"Here's the opening." Dick's voice was filled with relief.

Greta held tightly to his hand as he worked his feet down through the opening.

"Hey!" he yelled. "Hey! This isn't . . ."

As soon as he said it the pull on Greta's hand became too strong. He slipped from her grasp and was gone.

"Dick! Dick! What happened? Where are you? Are you in the Great Hall?"

There was no sound from Dick. Greta felt choked. The skin over her entire body prickled with new sensitivity. She could feel the flow of cold air currents she had not noticed before. She had only one thought . . . to find Dick. He might have been hurt!

Greta pushed her legs down into the hole, hung on to the edge as long as she could then. . . . . .
. . . "EEEEEEEEEH." She screamed as she began sliding down a steep muddy bank.

"Dick! Dick!" Her voice was tremulous. She had stopped sliding but the darkness prevented her from seeing what kind of a place it was. "Please, Dick please. Where are you?" It was as dark in this pit as in the one above but she knew it was not the Great Hall. That much she could tell by a sixth sense. They were working farther and farther into the cave . . . into the mountain.

Then Greta heard it. It was a high pitched note. She listened closely. It could not be Dick. No human being living could make a sound like that. The word "living" had popped uninvited into her mind, and how she wished it hadn't. She leaned

53

against the muddy bank in the total oblivion and heard the high pitched shriek with helpless terror. She felt about her. The cave was large. She could stand up. She started staggering around, walking, now half jogging over the uneven floor, blindly, almost hysterically.

As she walked, something brushed her. Something moving that scratched her face clawlike and brushed by with a floating motion. Greta wanted to cry out but her throat was closed tight. It was like a nightmare. She was trying to get somewhere and she could not get there and she wanted to scream and she couldn't. She slowed down and held her hands ahead of her. The cavern was narrowing. It was a cold light, without warmth and it silhouetted a many tentacled, moving shape, pulsating, flowing, growing, shrinking slowly . . . slowly.

It is! It is! The ghost of Augusta Guthrie. Greta could see the fluttering sunbonnet strings, the slowly billowing skirt . . . even . . . even . . . the glowing, empty eyes. Greta's hand flew to her mouth. She bit her lip in anguish and terror. She moved slowly backward, unable to turn her face away from the apparition that was reaching toward her . . . reaching . . . reaching.

As she backed along, the passageway grew smaller and she inched along the wall which turned suddenly.

"Oh!" Greta gasped with disbelief at what she saw.

It was a shaft of light. A thin, warm, oblique,

sun-born band, dancing with myriad dust motes suspended within it like an infinitesimal milky way.

"Oh!" Greta repeated and the relief she felt reached through her body and loosened the fear. She raced forward wildly to the ray of light. She found a small opening as she searched the rocks. It had a well-worn pathway with small footprints of what appeared to be a racoon. It was surprisingly easy to work her way out of the opening, which was covered thickly with mountain laurel. She worked through the bushes, scratching herself as she went. Then she glanced around quickly to see where she was. She was on the other side of the crest from the opening, on the low side of the bank. That's how there could be an opening to the surface even though they had gone deeper. She ran around the side of the hill as rapidly as she could and got a flashlight from the guide's shack near the mouth of the cave. In the early morning light she did not think of the ghost, but as she again approached the opening, she felt the fear swell within her. Pushing aside the bushes, she entered the same way she had come out. She hoped that the apparition had gone to other quarters because she did not know if she had courage to face it again. But she had to find Dick.

"Dick! Dick!" She cupped her hands to her mouth as she called. Then she heard a stumbling sound. "Greta, I'm here, I'm coming."

Forgetting about the apparition in her relief at hearing Dick's voice, she ran forward and then she saw it. An old piece of cloth hanging from a hole in the wall, fluttering with the breeze from the passageway to the outside. But the glow?

As she rounded the turn she saw Dick. He came down the corridor with a slight limp but with a smile spread all over his face. "Boy, am I glad to see you. That darned phosphorous deposit with that old rag flapping over it gave me quite a start. Some racoon or something put it in that hole, I'll bet. There's a lot of other junk from the trash barrels too, and look at all the animal tracks around it."

Greta led him quickly to the opening and his eyes lit up as though he were seeing a Christmas tree full of presents. "Say . . . good girl! This is something we can't keep secret. The Park Service hasn't the slightest idea there is another way out of the caves."

"Let's tell them about the whole thing." Greta's face glowed as she spoke. "It would be selfish to not let other people see that room you discovered. Let's call it The Chamber of Dark Flowers, O.K.?"

Dick grinned his acquiescence as though he appreciated her selection.

At last, scratched but happy, they were sitting on the ground outside the cave. The sun was coming over the horizon, evaporating the last residue of fear and giving courage with its golden touch.

"I've got to hand it to you, Greta, you've got what it takes."

"How do you mean? Finding the opening?"

"Yeah, that too. But I mean, you never once panicked about that ghost or anything. Cool as a hunk of ice all the way. Man, when I made that hand shadow on the cavern wall by holding my hand in front of a match, I darn near scared myself, it looked so bad. When a bat flew into me later I nearly jumped out of my hide."

"Bat!" Greta grimaced and her hands flew up to her face.

"That's what I said. Didn't you know there were bats in the caves? Couldn't you hear that high-pitched squeak?"

"Ooooh, no!" Greta twisted her mouth in disgust. "I'm glad I didn't know. Ghost are one thing but bats . . . boy!"

"You are crazy, Greta, crazy, crazy!" Dick grabbed her hand as they started trotting down the hill. "Hang on tight so you won't get lost," he said.

As they came closer to the clearing Greta glanced up the path to the boys' dormitory and saw it, or at least another one just like it. It was the shape she had seen before in the darkness. It was a doe, still black in the early dawn. It stood, hesitating a moment, then leaped into the brush beside the trail.

"Oh, look!" Greta was breathless. "That's what it was. When I was waiting for you this morning I thought you were a deer . . . or . . . I-I mean . . ."

Dick started laughing. "Gee thanks, I think you are pretty nice yourself."

"Oh, cut it out, Dick." Greta was embarrassed. "You know . . ."

But he was pulling her into a jogging run down

the twisting path. Then they were running faster and faster and laughing harder and harder as they neared the resort clearing below where the first smoke of the day rose thinly on the air.

The Ghost of
Old Stone Fort

◆━━━◆━━━◆━━━◆

HARRY HARRISON KROLL

DAD looked woefully at the flat on the old farm truck. "Well, young ones," he said, "looks like you're stuck here till about dusk. It's that patch on the inner tube. I saw a 'we-fix-flats' place out on the highway just before we turned down here to the fort. I'll carry the tube there and get it patched again, and you all stay around here till I get back." He pulled the tube out and thrust his arm through the limp thing.

Buddy, our youngest, looked frightened. "Reckon the Indian ghosts will catch us, Daddy?"

Dad came as close to glaring as he knew how. "Ghosts! Who's been filling your head with such nonsense?"

My sister Milly and I tried not to look guilty. But it had been good fun through the afternoon to pretend that the locality was haunted. My imagination took the lead but Milly's was not far behind. We'd pictured how it must have been at this strange

59

spot hundreds of years ago, when the Mound Builders had first settled and fortified this bend of the Elk River.

Dad pointed his finger at me. "No more of that. I'll be back as soon as I can. You can eat what's left in the lunch basket." He strode off, the last rays of the sunset falling upon him as he climbed the rise.

We got out the lunch basket from the truck and spread the remains of the food. It had been a very fine picnic. Just Dad and the three of us. Mother had gone down the country to visit Grandmother. We hadn't figured on the flat.

Buddy kept looking in all directions as the gloom thickened. He looked more like he wanted to cry than eat. We fussed at him. "Take this sandwich. Quit looking. Nothing here but us Indians." I laughed at my wit. Still and all, it was a spooky place. The Old Stone Fort was eerie enough by itself. Legend said it was even too old to be remembered by the redskins that used to be in here when Dad's family first settled this neck of the state. Some said the fort was built by De Soto's wandering Spaniards.

In any case it was quite a piece of doing. Nearly ten acres were enclosed in high stone and earth walls, with openings near the four corners which must have been protected by heavy timber gates. Maybe there were rude blockhouses at the corners for keeping tab on possible enemies. All that was gone, leaving nothing but the crude walls about as high in spots as a low house. It was so far back here in the swamp near the river that few people ever came this way, though the place was an old landmark. I had read about it in an old history book.

We'd planned to come here a long time. Now here we were, and night was shutting down.

When we finished the food Milly put the basket back, and the three of us made a huddle on an old army blanket. A night bird flew against the sky, making Buddy crawl up close to me.

"Boogars!"

"Boogars, your foot! It's a nighthawk."

"It's a redskin ghost!"

"Phooey!"

Milly said, "Jim, you ought not to have told all those crazy tales."

Dad should soon be returning. Instead the dark grew deeper. I listened to the sound of the waterfall, and the moan of the wind in the trees.

"I don't aim to live here even if Dad does buy the farm this thing's on!" Buddy declared.

"You'd better wait till Dad decides he wants to buy this forsaken old place," I shot back. Because, of course, that was one reason why we came here today. The farm with the fort was up for sale. There were six hundred acres and all except the land out on the highway were as stony and barren as this.

While we waited for Dad to come back through the gloom, we saw a funny thing. At first it looked no more than a candle light maybe ten miles away. If you have ever seen a candle flame that far in a pitch-black night, you get the idea. But instead of blowing out, the light increased, rose, began to spread, became more luminous. Buddy clutched me and hid his face and whimpered. Milly tried to console him, but she was scared too, and I admit my scalp began to crawl.

"It's nothing but a will-o'-the-wisp," I said, but I couldn't keep my teeth from chattering. The betrayal of my own fright scared Buddy and Milly all the more, for I was the one who was supposed to know things, or at least find out what I didn't already know.

Somehow this thing had me. I didn't know for sure what it was and I couldn't investigate. So the light grew and grew. It got up to about the tops of the low trees and stopped. It hovered this way and that a little, but the layer of air above acted like a roof and held it down. Then it began to spread to right and left. In no time at all it had taken the shape of two great big eyes. There it hovered, glaring right down at us. I just have to admit that I was scared till my mouth was bone dry. My judgment told me it was no ghost. But something else in me wondered if perhaps some Indian chief was hating this intrusion and was using the only weapon he had, his spirit, to chase us out.

Buddy began to wail dismally. "Let's get in the truck and leave this old place!"

"The truck's got a flat," I pointed to it.

"D-dadd-dd-yy!" Buddy moaned.

Milly shivered. I just sat glued to the army blanket.

"Why doesn't Daddy come on?" Milly half wept. "What's keeping him?"

"Maybe he couldn't find the flat-fixer. Maybe he saw the man who's fixing to sell the farm." There could be a lot of reasons.

Gradually then the eyes faded, spreading larger and wider and losing their shape almost completely. With a final blink and gulp the mystery eyes melted into the coming moonlight. And then Dad came back.

We fell on his neck, all babbling at once. He demanded, "Say, what's this all about?" I had the handiest tongue and I told him what we had seen. Buddy wept, "Let's get away from here," and I helped Dad put the inner tube in and pump up the tire. Soon we were loaded and riding from the spooky place. I was torn between two feelings: relief at getting away and curiosity as to just where the light had come from. Buddy huddled against Dad.

"You buy this old haunted place and I'll run away," he threatened.

"Ho!" Dad laughed. "Run away, eh? Where to?"

"Grandma's!"

Dad laughed again. I knew he was waiting for me to say something. "I did see the man who owns it. He'll sell. But if you kids are scared we won't think any more of it. I don't think too much of the farm anyhow. Most of it is rocks. The price is about the highest thing about it. Still, it's right nice here.

Good neighbors, they say. But it's sort of up to you young ones. You'll have to live here."

"I won't live here, I'll run away!" Buddy yelled.

"Calm down now; you won't have to live here then," Dad said.

We got home pretty late, and Buddy was asleep. The house seemed empty with Mother gone. It wasn't a very good house, and our farm was not a very good farm. Dad had a buyer on the string, however, and he wore his trading britches, and what we did would have to be done pretty fast. I went to sleep thinking about all this.

The next morning my mind was made up. "Dad, can I please use the truck today?"

"Why, son, what do you want with the truck?"

"I think I forgot something at Old Stone Fort."

"Forgot what?"

"To look for the bones of the ghost."

His eyes twinkled and he nodded. So I loaded up in the truck by myself. This was the kind of expedition I did best without having to explain what, if anything, was in the back of my head. The day was fair and sunny and beautiful. I felt free and happy. I always did when out on an adventure trying to explain away something that mystified me.

Though I started off with a great show of bravery, the closer I got to the old fort the more the marrow in my bones melted. At the stone road I turned off the highway. There stood Bos Moran, the man who was trying to sell the farm to Dad. He gave me a huge grin, and I had the feeling I was looking at a horse trader who would enjoy seeing me walk home. I couldn't guess what he thought I had come back for. I left him watching after me.

After lurching around a lot of sharp road bends I arrived once more at the fort site. I got out and looked the situation over. There was the ancient stone-and-earth work. I sat, remembering that legends told how most of this work was done by squaws. The Indian men might lay the foundations, but the filling in of thousands of jars of loose earth was done by the females. They must have been patient and unsavage creatures, to tote the loads of the mound builders.

The place was eerie even here in broad daylight. I could half close my eyes and see the braves marching the line of walls, of bloody men beating off an attack with savage glee. I imagined some last terrible engagement, in which the defenders at last were overcome and the braves killed and the old men and women put to the tomahawk and the young women, girls and children spared, to become members of the new tribe. It all gave me the most woozy feeling. Old Stone Fort deserved better than being forsaken like this. I kept wondering why the spot had never been developed into a state park. Such landmarks might last for generations, but something about them should be shared by people.

Finally I shook off my queer notions and made my way cautiously down to about where the big ghost eyes had come up out of the earth. It should have been spooky. There might at least have been sunken graves. But not a grave. I looked back under an outcropping of limestone, perfectly prepared to discover a lime-encrusted skull. Instead there was nothing but nut hulls where a rodent had denned up and fed.

The ground here, however, was plashy. It was at the top of a water table. Oozy springs collected and mint grew hereabouts. I could smell it. Below the limestone was a black kind of semi-stone. I scratched out some of it with my bare fingers and could crumple in my palm. Below ran the river.

In past days the rains had been heavy and I could see the flood mark on the stone. The high waters had been above the dark crumbly rock maybe a week past. I kept thinking about this. Maybe it had something to do with the ghost. Things were working in my mind but somehow they didn't drop into slots and click. I got a long stick and prodded back in the peat-like stuff. Then I lay flat on my stomach and investigated what looked like a small cave running back into the slope, down under the fort. All this did me no good.

But while I was here and had the time, and was alone—I loved being all by myself—I decided I would at least investigate the fort itself, and do more than rely on my imagination. I walked about, examining the stonework, I kicked loose shale, I climbed the high bank and looked in all directions. The waterfall was a steady supply of well-aired water. Below was a pool where the Indians and likely farm boys once swam. I could well imagine all this converted into a neat park, with bronze plaques instructing the curious passer-by what it was all about. I couldn't think of it as a private enterprise, though it could have been converted into something like that. A cabin for souvenirs and hotdogs. I could scour the countryside for arrowheads and other relics of forgotten stone-age men. If the weather was right, I might even produce a ghost!

I laughed right out at the foolish idea. And then it hit me right between the eyes. I hustled back down to the cave spot with the soggy peat. That was it. In my excitement I imagined I was my daddy and had a right to make a deal. I jumped into the truck and tore off back up the winding road and there was old Bos Moran looking as if he were waiting for me.

I yelled at him, "My daddy is going to buy your farm, Mr. Moran!"

He came to the big gate as I stopped. He grinned at me. "Yah, bub?"

"I'm sure he will," I hastily corrected myself.

"He didn't talk much like he would when he was fixing that flat tube."

"I know, but—"

"Did your pappy send you to tell me?"

"Not exactly, but—anyway, he'll be coming back maybe tomorrow and you can talk to him."

"It's got to be pretty fast talk."

I took off, because fast talk was just what I was thinking about. I really worried those old tires on the truck building up mileage. I was all out of breath like I had been running when I got home.

"Dad, I've been to Old Stone Fort and I think I

67

know where the eyes came from. I saw old Bos Moran and he said it would take fast talk. Well, let's talk fast—"

I rattled off my explanations of the ghost eyes, and Dad perked up. He agreed to go back in the morning, have a look around and talk with Bos Moran. He got some extra money to carry along. In the afternoon he talked with the neighbor about buying our small farm and came to a trade.

The next morning with a big basket of picnic we started off for Old Stone Fort again. Dad stopped by to talk with Mr. Moran. They agreed on a price. Dad took the money from his pocket and paid it for an option, to be taken up in a week. Then we rattled down to the fort. Buddy shivered and hid his face, but Milly was brave in the open daylight. We reached the parking place and got out. Buddy said at first he was going to hide under the blanket in the truck, but when we started off he decided he wanted to see what all the excitement was about, and came running. He hung to Dad's hand and we walked around the fort and came to the lower side. There at the dark pit we stopped.

"That's coal!" I made it sound dramatic.

Dad scoffed. "It's dead leaves and maybe old decaying trees, and peat."

"I know. That's ligneous coal. It's almost like wood. That's where the 'ghost' came from—phosphorous gas from the leaves and stuff that are decaying. The rise of the river wet it and made the ghost rise. Way back under there might be soft coal. But the important thing is the fort. We'd own it. Dad, we've just got to buy this fort. We can get the state park folks to come here and fix it up, and the state would build a road back in here, and we'd be written up in the papers—" I was all out of breath as my imagination pictured it.

Dad laughed, and then he became serious. "I don't know but what you have something, son. Okay," he decided. "If you all are not afraid of the spook, and if your mother likes the place—she will —then we can go ahead with the deal." So that was settled. We spent a terrific day here again, and I watched the misty ghosts with a feeling I owned them. It's lots more fun when you really own your own spooks.

Valley of No Return

WILLIS LINDQUIST

THE mountain slope lay green and sweet with the smells of spring. It seemed to please the tired sheep. Two weeks on the mountain trails had made them thin, but they were grazing contentedly now, as if they sensed that their summer grazing grounds had been reached at last.

The two Navajo boys hardly had time to notice their sheep. They looked in awe at a mountain pass about a mile away.

"That must be the entrance to the Valley of No Return," Yellow Hand told his young brother, Little Deer. "It doesn't look like much. I'm not afraid. Are you?"

Little Deer's eyes were very wide. He kept staring at the opening between the great red cliffs, remembering all the frightening Navajo legends about the valley.

Finally, he looked up at Yellow Hand. "They say those who go in never come out," he whispered.

"What happens to them? How can a whole flock of sheep disappear?"

Yellow Hand tried to laugh, but it did not sound like a laugh. "It's just some old Navajo superstition. Who ever heard of a valley that could swallow up herders and whole flocks of sheep?"

"All of us have heard it many times," Little Deer said. "It must be true. Grandfather said none of our people have dared to enter the valley for many years."

"Just superstition," Yellow Hand repeated. At school they say every superstition has a simple explanation."

Though Little Deer, too, had heard all about silly superstitions at school, he looked down at his feet and did not try to hide his uneasiness. "It is not good to live so near that evil place," he said.

"Where else could we find so much good grass?" Yellow Hand asked. During their two weeks on the trail with their sheep and their three calico ponies they had seen nothing nearly so good as this lush green slope. He looked up toward the mountains where the last spring snow still lingered on the sunny peaks. Far below them lay the brown sweep of the desert and red buttes standing like monuments to the time when the world was young.

"I don't like it," Little Deer said. "Look down there. That is the ledge Grandfather told us about, the place where the ancient ones of our people lie buried. Maybe this place is haunted."

Yellow Hand frowned. With good grazing land so hard to find these days, it did seem strange that this fine slope of grass was not being used. But he could not allow his young brother to see that he was puzzled.

He said, "You ought to be glad we found such a fine place. There is good soil for our corn. And look over there," he pointed. "People have lived here before. There is a hogan. It looks good enough to live in. Grandfather said there were three cisterns here for water. The ancient ones drilled them out of solid rock so they will last forever."

Leading their ponies, the boys approached the Navajo house. It was round and built out of stone and clay. As they entered, they saw the roof had caved in a little, making the smoke hole in the center larger than it should have been.

"Look!" Little Deer's voice caught. "Cooking pots, old clothes and rotten, old sheep pelts. Those who lived here must have left very suddenly—or something very bad happened to them."

Even Yellow Hand felt a chill brush up his spine. He did not like the look of this place, but he tried to be casual. "Old pots! Junk! Throw it all out. This place will do fine for the summer."

As he spoke, he edged over until his foot covered the perfect circle someone had scratched in the earthen floor. According to Navajo tradition, a closed circle, without a break in it for evil to drain out, was a bad sign, a curse. Someone had put it there as a warning.

Yellow Hand was glad Little Deer had not noticed it. The moment Little Deer went out with an

73

armful of rubbish, he rubbed the sign away with a stick.

He was responsible for his young brother. Ever since their mother and father had been lost in the big snow three years ago, their grandfather had looked after their flock of sheep. But now he was ill. He had sent them out for the summer, to make them strong, so that they could take their place with the men of the tribe and earn their own living. It was a test Yellow Hand could not afford to fail, for failure would bring shame and sadness to his grandfather.

As Yellow Hand looked over the place and examined the cisterns chipped out of solid rock, he wondered what strange thing had happened here. What had happened to the people who lived here a couple of years ago? Was there any real danger, or had they been frightened off by some ancient and foolish superstition?

Little Deer came up behind him so quietly that Yellow Hand almost jumped at the sound of his brother's breathing. "Why do you sneak up behind me that way?" he scolded. "We don't have time for any of your kid games."

"I wasn't sneaking up," Little Deer said. "I just figured out what happened to the people who were here. They must have taken their sheep into the Valley of No Return and just disappeared."

"Well, we don't have to take our sheep over there, so there's nothing to worry about."

But Yellow Hand knew the explanation wasn't

as simple as that because it did not explain the warning circle drawn on the floor of the hogan.

He was glad the cisterns had been left covered with a mat of branches. There was hardly any dirt in them at all. He was also glad that nothing unusual happened for several weeks.

They built brush corrals in which to keep their sheep and horses at night. With canvas buckets they filled the stone cisterns with water from the little mountain streams. Then the ewes began dropping their lambs as the slope became bright with spring flowers. As if by agreement, neither of them mentioned the mysterious Valley of No Return. Nor did they venture near it.

After the lambing period, the sheep had to be shorn. That was hard work. For want of wool soap, Yellow Hand dug roots of the yucca cactus, pounded and soaked the roots; the milky water in which they had soaked, washed the new wool white as bleached bones. Then the corn had to be put in. It was planted when the cornbird—the yellow-shouldered blackbird—came from the south, according to ancient Navajo tradition.

But all was not well. The spring rains they had been expecting did not come. Streams dwindled to trickles, then became dry washes on the mountain side. Day after day, they looked for rain clouds in vain. Soon they were forced to ration their precious cistern water.

"From now on we have to let the sheep out to graze before sunrise, so they can lick the dew from the grass," said Yellow Hand. "And we'll only give

75

them water from the cisterns every other day. We have to make the water last until we have more rain."

But he knew the water was not going to last very long with sixty head of sheep and three horses and two boys drinking it. The worst of it was that it was almost too late now for heavy spring rains to fall, and ahead of them stretched the normal, summer dry season. A feeling of hopelessness swept over him.

Upon the slope with his flock one afternoon, Yellow Hand was startled by a sound. Three times it came—the hoot of an owl in broad daylight. In spite of himself, he felt a tightening in his stomach. The hoot of an owl was said to bring bad luck. Three hoots, according to his grandfather, meant a dire warning.

He told himself this was merely another Navajo superstition. But superstitions lived with from childhood, he found, were not so easily put aside. During the next few days, for some reason he could not explain, he kept glancing up the slope time and again. It didn't make sense.

Then Little Deer seemed strangely frightened one evening. He pressed close to Yellow Hand as they drove their sheep into the brush corral.

"This—this place is evil," he said, his voice trembling. "It watches. It waits. It has eyes. We are never alone."

For a moment, Yellow Hand started at his brother. So Little Deer felt it, too? Then it wasn't merely his imagination. There was something dark, something frightening about this place that evoked an unknown fear.

To calm his small brother, he said, "Perhaps you don't like the space, the stillness here." He looked out over the vast desert. The amber light of the setting sun touched the buttes, changing them into frozen flame against blue distance. "We are valley people. That is the trouble. We'll get used to this bigness."

Little Deer refused to listen to that kind of talk. "I think Grandfather was right. This place is haunted. I heard sounds. Something moved there among the rocks today." He pointed down slope at the shelf where the ancient ones were buried.

The tightness came into Yellow Hand's stomach again. Could the place really be haunted? Was that why the others had left so suddenly, why they had scratched a closed circle on the floor of the hogan?

"I don't want to stay here any longer," Little Deer said. "Please, Yellow Hand, take me home."

"If we went home now our sheep would die on the way. And everyone would laugh at us and say we were afraid of the dark. Grandfather would be so ashamed he would not find words to say to us for many days. When Grandfather said this place was haunted, he meant to test our courage."

Yellow Hand walked away before his brother could answer him. They could not go back. That was impossible. But their corn had withered and died as it came from the ground. Now the grass was turning brown on the slopes.

All his wonderful dreams for a good summer were fading to nothing. If rain did not come within a week their water would be gone and their sheep would die.

His sleep was troubled that night. Once he sat up with a start, suddenly alert. He saw the embers of their fire glowing softly beyond the doorway. Some sixth sense told him they were not alone. Yet, he heard nothing but the small sounds from the sheep corral, and the deep, steady breathing of his younger brother.

Carefully he rose, picked up his rifle, and inched toward the open door. There was no moon, only the bright stars. Not a breath of air stirred. It was so still that the silence of the night seemed to press against him. For several minutes he watched and listened, then moved slowly to the corral and the cisterns.

As he came around the hogan on his way back he stumbled against something. His fingers touched the familiar framework of his saddle—and his breath caught. The saddle had been moved! Someone or something had been here. It was the kind of senseless thing that was supposed to happen in haunted places.

He took up a position near the door and huddled there, waiting and watching till dawn touched the eastern sky with tints of gold.

Later, in the bright morning sunlight, he thought he saw the faint imprint of a moccasin near the loom. Armed with his rifle, he took his flock down the slope to the ancient burial grounds. If Little Deer had seen movement down there, it might be possible to find tracks.

He found many. They were all made by the same cracked pair of moccasins. Here and there rocks had been removed from the graves, so the men could get at the precious treasures of silver and turquoise buried with the dead.

The grave robber had clearly been working this rich burial ground for several years. No wonder he did not want anyone living on the slope above. By haunting the place he'd been able to drive people away without arousing suspicion. In that way he never ran the risk of being reported to the reservation police, who would have come in swarms and made short work of him.

Yellow Hand suddenly became aware that his sheep were behaving strangely. They had not had any water that morning, which always made them more restless than usual. But now they seemed on the verge of panic.

Their loud bleating must have covered the first faint rumble from above. But suddenly Yellow Hand heard it and turned to see several boulders come hurtling down the mountain side.

The bounding rocks seemed to gather speed as they came. They narrowly missed the hogan. On they came, straight at him and the sheep; the sheep broke into a run. Just in time, he drove them aside, and the rocks went thudding harmlessly by.

The sudden attack left him breathless and hollow

inside. Someone had tried to kill him, or at least to drive him away. He was relieved to see Little Deer come on the run.

"Stay with the sheep," he gasped. Quickly, he told his young brother what he had discovered. "The grave robber must have seen me come down here and knew I'd see him work. He'll kill us if he can to keep us from reporting his crimes." He waved his rifle toward the shelf where the rocks had started. "I'm going up there."

He walked westward along the slope. It would be hard to surprise the grave robber, but he had to get the man quickly before he could strike again.

He dropped into a dry ravine which concealed him from view, and followed it straight up the slope. Well over an hour had passed before he reached the ledge. There were fresh tracks, and places where rocks had been wedged loose. With his rifle at ready, he searched behind every projection where a man might hide, but found nothing. The man was gone.

The distant report of a shot drew him to the edge of the shelf. He looked down the empty slope. Little Deer and the sheep were nowhere in sight.

To the left his eyes caught a movement. It was a smudge of dust such as a flock of sheep would raise; it was moving steadily toward the Valley of No Return.

For once, Yellow Hand was willing to believe in the terrible dangers of the mysterious valley. He bounded down the slope at an angle to get ahead of them. The grave robber had outsmarted him and struck again. This time he meant to dispose of Little Deer, who was unarmed, and the sheep by driving them into the valley.

It soon became apparent to Yellow Hand that he would be much too late to head them off. But if he had a horse his chance would be improved. Sliding down a draft of shale, he made for the corral.

Long minutes passed before he had the warmth of horse flesh under him. Then flying hoofs beat out a rhythm that kept pace with his heart. He shuddered to think of the terrible things that might happen to Little Deer if he lost this race.

His horse galloped on, quartering the slope, plunging into ravines and out again, with Yellow Hand hunched low over the pony's neck.

But their speed was not enough. When they came within sight of the valley's entrance, only a haze of ascending golden dust hung between the sheer umber cliffs. Little Deer and the sheep had already passed beyond to an unknown doom.

A shot rang out as he started between the cliffs. His pony reared in fright. Yellow Hand pitched headlong into the dust. He rolled, made a grab for his rifle and dashed for cover as a bullet keened over his head.

The shots were coming from a crevice halfway up the cliff. And ahead he caught a glimpse of sheep as they went up the valley. In desperation he shouted for Little Deer to turn them back.

Piercing laughter answered him from the cliff. The crevice in which the man was hiding made perfect cover so long as Yellow Hand faced it at an angle. But it would become a death trap if he could reach a position in front of it and shoot in.

He worked deeper into the valley entrance by diving from rock to rock. Every move he made drew the grave robber's fire. Bullets began whipping dangerously close as the man learned to anticipate his every move, until at last even the slightest feint brought a shot or two.

The man was becoming desperate, using a lot of ammunition. That was all to the good. But precious minutes were passing. If Little Deer and the sheep were to be saved there wasn't much time left— probably only seconds.

Yellow Hand looked ahead for another rock behind which he could take cover. But there were no more rocks, no cover of any kind. He hesitated. To run across open ground meant almost certain death. Yet he had to go on. He had to reach Little Deer before anything happened to him.

Perspiration rolled down his face as he raised himself enough for a peek at the crevice where the man was hiding. To his surprise he found he could almost look into it now. And stranger still, the man was not shooting. Had he run out of ammunition?

Then he saw the man trying to scale an almost vertical wall. As Yellow Hand watched in horror, he knew the man wasn't going to make it. He heard the scream, saw the man's body wheel into space and come plunging down to death on the rocks below.

Yellow Hand, suddenly free, ran at top speed up the valley. It seemed to be empty. He saw nothing but the vast rock walls looming in eternal silence. His shouts brought no answer.

The broad trail of the flock led him to a yawning cavern in the upper end of the valley. There several lambs had been trampled to death as the sheep had struggled to enter the cavern.

For the space of several seconds Yellow Hand stood rooted, too stunned to move. Waves of numbness passed over him. He had come too late. The ancient stories were true. The evil valley had swallowed his brother, his flock of sheep, all that counted!

Slowly, like one in a daze, he entered the cavern. He felt a cool flow of air in his face, and the air had the smell of water. Suddenly he understood the terrible secret of the valley. Only the smell of water could have made sheep struggle so desperately to enter. He knew how Little Deer must have tried to get in front of them to turn them back, how the sheer weight of their numbers had forced him in.

Yellow Hand made a torch, lighted it and again entered the darkness of the cavern. Here several more sheep had been trampled in the flock's surge toward water.

The underground tunnel turned left after several yards and suddenly Yellow Hand came to a sheer drop of five or six feet. Little Deer and the flock had fallen into the rushing black water directly below, and the underground river had carried them off.

Staring at the black water, Yellow Hand felt the tears gathering in his eyes.

But suddenly he heard something that made his pulse quicken. Dropping to his knees he listened intently. The sounds were unmistakable now. Above the rumbling of the river he could hear the clear, sweet tinkle of bells and the faint bleating of sheep. And the miracle of it was that the sounds were coming from upstream!

Yellow Hand lost no time in dropping into the rushing water. It was only ankle deep. Thanks to the dry season the river was low and the sheep had not been swept to their death. They were going upstream, toward the fresh flow of air. And Little Deer was sure to be with them.

How long he followed the river tunnel, he did not know. It seemed endless. But always ahead he could hear the faint sounds of the sheep. Now the smell of growing things came on the flowing air, and at last he saw the dim light of day up ahead.

He came out into a sunny valley completely surrounded by mountains. There was a sparkling blue lake in the center, which fed the river. On all sides were fresh green slopes where his sheep were grazing.

Little Deer came running, his face masked with fear. "That man——"

"You don't have to worry about him. He won't be troubling us any more." Yellow Hand looked up at the high pine slopes. He saw a pass in the mountains, through which they could come and go. He laughed, and raised his arms wide. "All ours, Little

Deer. In our secret valley we'll have food and water as long as we live."

"Are we going to bring grandfather here when he gets well?"

"Yes," Yellow Hand said. "Grandfather will see us as men now. He'll be glad to come. After all, this valley belongs to him, too. If he hadn't sent us out for the summer to test us in his old-fashioned way, we would never have found this place at all."

Little Deer smiled. "And if he begins talking about superstitions, we'll just let him talk and be happy."

Mystery of the
Ghost Junk

◆━━◆━━◆━━◆━━◆

JAMES BENEDICT MOORE

RIDING out the great ocean swells of the Japan Sea as he stood in the bow of their sailboat, Bill was the first to catch the ominous sound of the threatening wind and the dark water rushing with typhoon force upon them.

The three of them—Bill Maxwell, his younger brother Carl, and their companion, Kats Sato— were returning with supplies for their camp on Arako Island, forty miles off Yokohama. They were to join their father, Dr. Walter Maxwell, and Kats' father, Dr. Kwanjiro Sato, in a few hours, bringing much needed food and equipment for continuing the expedition the two archaelogists had begun ten days before.

Bill leaped aft now, moving his big frame like one long accustomed to living aboard ship.

"Carl, Kats! Quick, bring her about into the wind!"

Bill got only as far as amidships when the smashing wind caught them. They were sailing before the wind with sail full out.

"Carl!"

In his confusion, the twelve-year-old at the tiller moved the heavy stick toward him, causing the edge of the sail to be caught by the violent gust of wind.

Bill ducked and scrambled on hands and knees as Kats moved to loosen the jib sheet.

"Look out, you idiot, we're going to jibe!"

With a noise like the crack of a gun the sail went around. Then there was a tortured splinter as the terrifying force of the wind carried the mast, sail, boom, and rigging all into the foaming water.

The tiny ship fought for air and came up half filled with water.

Bill felt a furious anger at what the clumsy seamanship of his younger brother had caused. There was no time for that now. He saw Kats—although he could not hear him—yelling for help amidships. The main sheet had caught him about the waist and the weight of the rigging gone overboard was about to pull him from the boat.

Carl crawled forward, handing his brother a sheath knife. Both of them tugged and hacked until they got Kats free.

Bill yelled at them between showers of spray which were filling the boat even deeper with dark green water.

"Start bailing!"

Kats caught his arm and Bill saw his dark face

grimace as he pointed forward. Where the mast step had been was a gaping hole in the hull as big as two fists.

Bill remembered their life jackets and started digging them out from under a seat. As they were strapping them on there was a cry from Carl.

"Look, Bill, what's that?"

They turned in the direction he pointed.

A large craft—in a second they made it out as a junk—was bearing straight down on them. Its sails were furled.

They caught Bill's intention in a flash as he splashed towards a coil of rope.

He shouted into the spray-soaked faces.

"Get a weight . . . there . . . that canteen!"

Quickly he tied the canteen strap to the end of the rope.

"Let's get a rope around her mast!"

The junk was nearly upon them, its huge high-peaked prow curling the water on either side. It would miss their sinking boat by only a few yards.

Bill flung the rope out and they saw the canteen go twirling around the bare mast. All three of them scrambled to catch the rope as it slithered out of its coil.

Bill grabbed for the end and wound it about him. He yelled at them.

"Overboard, quick! You two ahead of me . . . got to get on that junk!"

They were all in the boiling sea, fighting for their lives then.

Bill felt the rope tighten about his chest until it

seemed it would cut him in two. He saw Carl's blond head, then Kats', ahead of him. Good, they were both on the line.

"Kats," he yelled. "Stay with Carl. I'll get to the ship and pull you in."

The last thing he saw as he surged forward was Kats slipping back to circle his strong brown arms around the younger boy.

Somehow his strength managed to hold out while Bill pulled himself to the side of the careening junk and hauled himself aboard the slippery deck. He could not see his two companions at the end of the long line now. Its tautness made him sure they were there.

He banged his fist on the cabin, calling out as he did so. His yell was swept from his lips. If there was anyone aboard, he had not heard Bill. With a cry of thankfulness, as he crawled forward on hands and knees, Bill spotted the anchor winch, a fat line still tugging at it and running overboard into the sea. Seizing the line he had thrown, which was still twisted securely about the mast, he wrapped it around the winch and began to turn the handles. In a moment he gave a thankful shout. The heads of Carl and Kats came into sight astern.

Bill set the winch with a pin, which hung there on its chain, and ran to the side of the junk. He grasped the exhausted Carl half by the hair and half by the shirt, pulling him to the deck.

Kats was half way up the rope when Bill returned to assist him aboard. In another moment

90

he had flung open the heavy door to the junk's cabin and they were inside, the door latched against the roaring sea.

Kats pounded Bill in his relief and found words at last.

"Wow, Bill, how did you get the line in?"

"I used the anchor winch." He turned to his brother. "Are you okay, Carl?"

The twelve-year-old grinned a sickly green grin.

"Yeah . . . I guess so . . . just full of salt water, that's all."

Kats got up and began examining the cabin lockers and table.

"Hey Bill, Carl. No crew. How come? Where's the crew on this junk?"

"You got me," said Bill. "There is no one aboard, as far as I can make out."

They all stood—Carl unsteadily—and joined Kats in his search of the cabin. They soon knew they were on no mere fisherman's junk from the expensive furnishings and fittings everywhere.

"Look at this—canned goods and a real stove. And look at that—fuel supply lines. This must be a motor junk."

"Yeah," replied Bill. "It must have been swept out to sea in this storm. The anchor line and mooring lines are still dragging overboard."

Carl sat down again on the matted floor, looking paler than ever.

"Were we lucky this junk blew our way. What would we have done?"

His question went unanswered, the other two not wanting to think of that.

They started removing their life jackets, and Kats discovered some dungarees and shirts in a cabin locker.

Kats—whose full name was Katsumi—looked at Bill as if expecting the older boy to volunteer suggestions.

At seventeen, Bill Maxwell was considered their leader—when they were not with the two archaeologists they had left on tiny Arako Island—while they returned to Yokohama for provisions.

Kats was fifteen, in public school in Tokyo and an inseparable companion of the two brothers, who attended classes at Tokyo American School and had come to Japan six years before when their father came to the faculty of Tokyo Imperial University.

They sat silently for a few minutes. Bill thought of Dr. Sato's instructions as they planned the expedition to Arako in search of evidences of the Tanshiro Dynasty which five hundred years ago had moved its court in exile to the island.

"Do not broadcast our destination, please, boys," Dr. Sato had said. *"I will explain later."*

Kats, practical as usual, broke the silence.

"Well, let's not sit here. I'm getting hungry. I volunteer as cook if I can find something in those cans worth eating and can get the stove going."

Bill grinned at him.

"A good idea, Kats. I'll have a look at the engine and see if I can get it started. But there's not much use trying to do anything until this storm blows over. . . ."

"How far do you think we are from Arako by now?"

"Hard to say," said Bill. "As far as I can make out this storm came out of the south. Therefore it should be blowing us towards the island—or even past it. But . . . we shouldn't be too far away."

Kats was already banging around at the stove and they saw he had an oil burner lit and was piling up some cans.

"Hey, Bill," said Kats. "I still think it's funny there was no crew on board. This isn't a fishing junk. Looks like a sort of private yacht—maybe a businessman's pleasure junk. But you'd think they would leave a crew on board. She must be a good fifty feet in length. A terrific boat!"

"Isn't there some law of the sea that says the finders of a boat adrift can keep it," Carl said.

His brother got up and started out of the cabin.

"Something like that, Carl. That would be some catch, all right, if we could keep it for ourselves."

"I hope Dad and Dr. Sato are okay." Carl spoke the thought uppermost in the minds of each of them.

"Oh, they probably had the tents blown down on them and got a good soaking," said Kats, speaking from the end of the cabin where the odor of canned meat heating in a pan was beginning to drift through the cabin. "But they'll be all right."

"I'm going around to the wheelhouse and down

to the engine room—if there is an engine room," Bill said. "I'll be right back."

Carl got up and started to follow, but his brother said, "You better stay in where it's dry, Carl. Help Kats with that grub, and you guys go ahead and eat."

Bill fought against the cabin door, and once he got on deck the wind snatched its handle from his grasp and slammed it shut. The sky was still dark with storm winds, and mountainous waves pounded over the sturdy junk from stem to stern.

He found the wheelhouse and navigator's table in it as snug and tidy as if the boat had been anchored in harbor. The wheel was secured with ropes which creaked at every fierce tug of the waves on the rudder. The compass by the wheel confirmed his guess—they were being blown almost due north.

A chart, fixed on the table, was of an enlarged section of Yokohama Bay. A cursory examination showed him the island of Arako—where they had left his father and Dr. Sato three days before—was plainly marked. There were many other islands shown on the chart and markings had been scratched across it with a pen.

He went down the steep companionway to what he guessed must be the engine room, saying to himself, if we can figure out how to get this thing going we'll be okay.

He was not surprised to find the powerful, grey-enameled diesel in the engine room in as shipshape a condition as the rest of the boat. Stooping to examine a panel of instruments he pressed what he guessed was a starting switch. Instantly he heard a motor go into action and the chug of the diesel turning over. The engine did not start, however. He was satisfied they could start the engine once the proper switches were thrown in the wheelhouse.

He made his way back to the cabin, picking up the topmost chart in the wheel house on the way.

Kats hailed him, picking up a tin plate and going to the stove.

"About time you got back . . . another five minutes and we'd have eaten your food, too. We were starved."

Bill saw his brother had more color in his face.

"Feeling better, Carl?"

"Yeah, that canned meat wasn't bad. I didn't know Kats could cook like *that*."

The younger boy looked sober. "I'm sorry I jibed the *Westwind,* Bill, really. it was awfully stupid."

Bill shook his head. "Forget it."

He saw Kats nodding in agreement.

"If we hadn't been dismasted right then we might have missed this junk . . . and . . . I hate to think what would have happened to us trying to make Arako in this storm."

Kats stepped over to pick up the chart Bill had dropped on the floor, steadying himself against the bulkhead as the boat gave a tremendous lurch.

"Will the engine start, Bill?"

"I think so—yeah. There's juice in the batteries."

Bill came over and got down on his hands and knees over the chart.

"Isn't that Arako Island, Kats?"

He placed a finger on the chart at the location of a tiny island, as they were joined by Carl.

"Sure, that's Arako," said Kats, reading the Japanese printing.

Bill shifted his finger to an even tinier island, quite a way to the south.

"What's this one called?"

"Konshu."

"That's what I thought. Your father mentioned we might go over there exploring sometime if the tide was right. Kats, what are these circles and words in Japanese?"

Bill pointed to the markings on the seaward side of both the islands which had words printed in a tiny, neat Japanese script.

Kats squinted at the writing.

"It's the word for . . . station . . . or, what would you say in English? It means station or literally translated . . . deposit . . . depository."

"Depository," said Bill and Carl together, studying the chart a moment longer.

"Do you think it has something to do with fishing, maybe?" said Carl.

"I doubt it. This isn't a fishing vessel we're on. And the tide off Arako and Konshu makes fishing poor there."

They were all silent; the only sound in the stuffy cabin was the pounding of the sea against the hull.

"I wonder what it could mean," said Bill.

Kats indicated the scores of small islands dotting the outer rim of Yokohama Bay.

"Most of these islands are mere rocks in the sea, you know. From what Father has told me, no one lives on most of them. I don't know what these marks for stations would mean here."

Bill studied Kats' face.

"Why did your father warn us not to say anything about where we were going on this expedition?"

"I always thought it was because as an archaeologist, Father was so keen for making original discoveries and didn't want others at rival universities to find out what he'd learned about these islands."

"Could he have any other reason?" asked Carl. "Why were we supposed to light a fire every other night on the beach at Arako, so the Coast Guard patrol would know everything was okay?"

Bill looked skeptical.

"I never did get a straight answer out of Dad on that one. He said it was just so the Coast Guard could keep tabs on us—but why they want to do that with a harmless rockpickers expedition, I don't know."

Kats got up and stared out a porthole.

"Waves are getting smaller," he said. "Let's see if we can get that engine going."

The three of them went out and along the deck to the wheelhouse.

"Throw those switches there," said Bill, "as soon as I yell from the engine room."

In five minutes they had the powerful diesel sending the junk solidly into the cross waves; and when Bill came up the companionway, he saw that Kats was already at the wheel while Carl was loosening the lines which secured it.

Kats spoke over his shoulder, studying the compass.

"What do you guess our direction is to Arako?"

"We've been out of Yokohama since six this morning. It's now about three o'clock, I'd guess. I think this storm must have blown us past Arako, so I'd say a course almost directly east by southeast would hit the island. But," concluded Bill lamely, "that's a small island in a big sea. That's only my guess."

"East by southeast it is," called Kats, spinning the wheel to starboard and causing the boat to heel far over as it began to buck the heavy seas.

"We ought to get more speed out of her than this," said Carl, fiddling with the levers at the side of the binnacle. They heard the engine roar to fuller life and felt the dig of the propellers as he advanced one of the levers.

"That's more like it," said Bill. "I'm going below to see if I can check on the fuel supply. Keep her steady on course, Kats."

About two hours later Carl had gone to the cabin to make some supper and Kats and Bill were staring anxiously ahead in the rapidly gathering dusk, searching for a sign of Arako Island.

They heard the cabin door bang and then a yell from Carl.

"Hey, you landlubbers, land ho!"

They turned to look off the portside and recognized at once the low, dark silhouette of Arako with its white sand beach.

Kats swung the boat to port as Carl called.

"If you guys would look in the right direction you might get us there yet."

Bill grinned.

"Okay, captain!" Then he said to Kats, "I guessed we had drifted farther north than we had. We nearly sailed right by it."

They were rapidly nearing the island now, and Bill yelled back to reply to Carl's supper call.

"Let's wait until we anchor."

"We'll have to take the dinghy ashore. It wouldn't be safe to beach this boat, would it?"

In another few minutes the white sand on the beach gleamed luminously beyond the short breakers. In the bow, poised ready to let go the spare anchor they had brought up from a forward hatch, Bill and Carl peered anxiously for a glimpse of their camp and any sign of their father and Dr. Sato.

Carl gave a sharp whistle, then called, "Hey, Dad, Doctor Sato, we're back!"

The only sound was the recurring wash of the waves on the almost completely dark beach.

Bill stared anxiously at his brother, then yelled at Kats as the sand beach was suddenly right before them.

"Send her around and kill the engine!"

At the same instant he released the anchor winch, sending the heavy anchor plunging into the shallow water. The boat swung slowly until the stern faced the shore a scarce fifty yards from the beach. Bill and Carl were joined by Kats, and they proceeded to go amidships and untie the dinghy, then throw out a small stern anchor and tighten the line.

Kats said, "Okay, let's go."

They hoisted the dinghy over the side and rowed rapidly to the beach. The first one out of the boat, Carl started to run through the surf ahead of them, and Bill called after him.

"Let's go together, Carl; I don't like the looks of things."

In the near darkness, as they approached the camp site, signs of the storm's destruction were visible. Branches from the scrub pines were strewn about the beach. The long grasses at the edge of the beach were flattened and soaked by the rain.

Carl started to run again as they cleared the rise above the sand.

"I see the tents. They're both down. Dad! Doctor Sato, can you hear us!"

The three of them reached what had been a neatly arranged camp of two good sized tents and an array of camping paraphernalia. It was now a jumble of soggy canvas and archaeologists' tools, with lanterns and cots thrown in a wet heap. There was no light, no message, no sign of their fathers.

In the almost complete darkness the three boys stood close together, the only sound on the tiny island coming from their heavy breathing and the roar of the surf below.

"I simply can't understand it," Bill broke their disheartened silence at last.

"Dad and Dr. Sato must be on this island somewhere."

"Maybe they sought shelter from the storm somewhere else," said Kats, not sounding very convincing.

"It's possible." Carl tried to make out the faces of Kats and his older brother in the pitch darkness.

"But it's too dark to search now—and our lanterns all seem to be on the blink."

Bill started down toward the shore.

"Let's go aboard and get a night's rest. We'll make a search of the island first thing in the morning."

Once aboard the trim motor junk they got into warmer clothes and turned on the boat's lanterns and stove in the cabin, deciding they would take turns standing watch for four hours each. In a locker in the wheelhouse Kats came upon a regular arsenal of pistols and rifles. He trembled with the thought of their significance.

"I'm sure this isn't a fishing junk now," he said, "and as for it being a businessman's pleasure craft —I doubt that too . . ."

He saw that Bill, who had come up on deck behind Carl, was giving him the sign to knock off, so he was quiet.

Bill was not surprised to find his brother, who

had been given the first watch, slumped in exhausted sleep on the afterdeck when he came up at midnight.

When Kats and Bill were ready to start their search of the island after an early breakfast, Bill suggested that Carl stay aboard and keep watch. He knew his brother was still dog-tired from the preceding day's experience.

When they began their swing around the island, Bill turned to Kats. "I don't like the looks of this at all, Kats. There's something fishy about the whole thing. I didn't want to say anything in front of Carl. But there's some danger on these islands we don't know about, and Dad and your father did. Isn't that the reason for the signal lights at night?"

Kats screwed up his face as he swung along. "I'd come to the same conclusion, Bill. Remember last night—when we found all those guns aboard?"

"Yeah—when I shut you up?"

"Yes. The boat and the guns and the marks on the two islands"—he paused—"our fathers' disappearance. Somehow, all these things could be related."

Bill stopped suddenly. "Kats! You said the Japanese word was *depository*. Smugglers, is that it?" Did we get aboard a boat from a smugglers' fleet which was set adrift by the storm?"

"It's well known the Coast Guard is always running down opium smugglers," said Kats. "It's brought in from the China mainland. But—remember—the marking for a station was on the seaward side of Arako Island. There's nothing here but cliffs and jagged rocks—no anchorage at all."

It was a small island—only three miles around —and Kats and Bill returned toward the blown down camp an hour later without having spotted a living thing except a flock of sea gulls, and without having seen a single sign of human activity.

"They must have been taken off by the Coast Guard," was Kats' discouraged conclusion as they approached the beach, hot and dusty from their hike.

"Yeah," Bill tried to disguise a feeling of fear, "and are probably frantically searching the bay for one small American sailboat named *Westwind*. What do you think we'd better do, Kats? I'd say beat it to Yokohama as fast as possible and hope we pick up the Coast Guard on the way."

"I don't know," said Kats. "If the signal fire was lighted night before last—assuming our fathers were still here then—the fire not lighted tonight would bring in the Coast Guard. But . . ."

"Yes, *but*, is right," said Bill. "After that storm the regular patrol may be a hundred miles from here towing in fishing craft. They've probably forgotten all about us by now."

Kats lifted his arm, pointed toward camp.

"Hey! That's smoke coming from camp!"

They ran forward, and at the same moment saw the lone figure of Carl standing up by a campfire he had going.

He shouted and waved something at them as

they came up. They saw the tents had been un-pegged and folded.

"Bill, Kats, here's a note; I found a note under Dr. Sato's tent!"

Kats took the water-spotted, smeared note pad, on the top leaf of which was scribbled almost illegibly *Konshu, Tanaka*.

"That's father's writing—looks like it was written in great haste. He's usually much neater."

"Konshu—that's the island south of here marked on the chart in the junk," said Bill.

"That's right," Carl joined in. "What's the *Tanaka* for, do you know?"

They looked at Kats.

"I don't know. It's a common Japanese name. . . but . . . I can't think of any reason for his putting it here."

"Kats, do you think this was a note left for us—or just the beginning of some notes your father was making?"

"Hard to say," Kats replied. "I do know it was made in haste. Father never writes like this when he's making research notes. He's very neat you know."

"Did you find any signs—any other messages or anything?" asked Bill.

"I went through everything," Carl said. "As far as I can see this camp was all set up when they left."

Bill stared out at the open sea. Carl moved to the fire and stirred a large kettle of canned beans heating there.

Konshu, thought Bill. *Just why would he write that?*

While they were in the midst of eating, Kats lowered a spoonful of beans and looked at them.

"I have a feeling Father was trying to tell us something—something he had to put down in a hurry. They were going to Konshu, maybe."

Bill snorted.

"Going to Konshu. But how? Swim? The island's forty miles from here. And surely the Coast Guard hasn't been around giving free rides. They wouldn't just up and leave camp and . . ."

"Coast Guard . . . Tanaka! I got it!" Kats waved his arms. "The head of the South Bay patrol—Captain Hiroshi Tanaka."

Carl and Bill stared at him.

"Is that his name?" Bill was confused.

"I'm positive," Kats said. "Now—what did Father mean? Going with Tanaka to Konshu. Or—tell Tanaka to come to Konshu. Or . . . something like that."

Bill jumped up, a new look of hope on his face.

"I think you've got it. If you ask me, the answer to our problem is on that island. We've got a good boat. We're armed. I say, let's sail for Konshu at once and forget about going back to Yokohama."

Carl was kicking dirt over the fire. He looked at his brother with a worried expression on his face.

"What do you mean by saying we're armed, Bill? You guys know something you aren't telling me."

Bill saw Kats shake his head in the affirmative.

105

"Okay, Carl, it's just this. We didn't want to get you worried when you were so tired last night. We think . . . well maybe there's some danger in these waters we don't know about—smugglers maybe!"

"You think the marks on the junk's chart may have something to do with smuggling?"

"There's a possibility."

They were ready to shove off—having stowed all the camp gear aboard the junk—when Bill remembered the name on Dr. Sato's scribbled note.

"We'd better leave a message in case the Coast Guard does land," he said.

He motioned to Kats and picked up the side of a packing case which had contained meat tins, then got a pencil stub from the last of the duffel bags.

He dictated to Kats who wrote in Japanese—*Dr. Maxwell and Dr. Sato missing*—"Let's see, this is July . . . twenty-ninth . . ." *when we returned from Yokohama July 28. Left July 29 for Konshu Island in search. Send Coast Guard to Konshu at once. Katsumi Sato, Bill and Carl Maxwell.*

The run to Konshu Island would take about three hours, Bill knew, with the sturdy craft he was piloting making about fifteen knots. That would get them to the island about the middle of the afternoon.

He looked out now on the calm sea as the shape of Arako receded on the stern horizon and sensed in the ominous oily calm of the water a warning of another storm such as the one which had dismasted the *Westwind* only two days previously.

He felt tired and discouraged, his anxiety concerning the whereabouts of his father and Dr. Sato only slightly lightened by the knowledge that the three of them were still together and that they had a sea-worthy, well-provisioned boat beneath their feet.

They had not been under way a half hour before he saw the gusts of wind coming out of the south starting huge swells in the calm ocean. In another ten minutes he rang the ship's bell loudly, bringing Carl and Kats on deck. He stuck his head out a wheelhouse window, getting a nose full of the foul, fishy smell of a typhoon sea.

"We've got another big blow coming, Kats. Can you guys secure the dinghy and those hatches?"

Kats yelled back at him, "Can we make the island?"

"The wind's directly out of the south again," Bill called. "I'll have to hold her nose to the waves if they get too big. That'll throw us off course about ten degrees—but we ought to make it by night with any luck."

Minutes later Kats and Carl dashed along deck and joined Bill as the first of the big waves smashed on the starboard bow and Bill swung the wheel to meet the next one head on. The boat dove so steeply the three of them were thrown together at the front of the wheelhouse.

The sky was the color of ashes now and the violent wind sent rivers of water smashing over the boat.

Bill slowed the engine until they were just making headway.

He yelled at his companions above the noise of the storm.

"We'll be hours late making Konshu. We can't land anyway until this blow calms down. You and Kats get some grub ready—and Kats, look at that chart and see where the landing is marked, will you?"

When Kats came on deck to relieve Bill at the wheel it was nearly five o'clock. Bill raised a hand in the direction of the sky to indicate the first signs of clearing weather. The foul smell of the stormy sea was still evident but the waves had receded to long swells again.

Bill swung the wheel over, turning the boat east.

"Keep her straight east, Kats, will you?"

He relinquished the wheel wearily, wondering how accurate they were.

"I'm guessing we've made it far enough south. A couple hours on that course ought to see Konshu somewhere in sight."

Bill went below to join Carl, who handed him a cup of hot coffee and showed him the approach to the island Kats had marked on the chart.

The clanging of the ship's bell—less than half an hour later—called them on deck in surprise.

Looking in the direction Kats was pointing from the wheelhouse they saw a tiny speck of land off the port quarter.

The swells in the dark gray sea were still large but the wind was dying.

"We must have made better time than you thought," Kats said, when they joined him at the wheel.

It was growing dark fast, and they knew they would be lucky to make Konshu before night closed in.

Bill took the wheel, moving the engine lever to full speed ahead.

He looked grimly at Kats and Carl.

"Get the anchors and dinghy ready, and . . . I guess we better get those guns loaded, too, and see that they're in good working order."

With all his concern about what the next hour would bring, Bill had to smile when he caught the picture of his brother coming on deck wearing a huge pistol strapped in its holster around his waist.

Kats came forward bringing the chart and Bill turned the boat around the north end of the island, whose dark hump could now be clearly seen in outline against the twilight sky.

"I don't see any lights. The landing—or whatever it is—marked on the chart is right here," Kats pointed at the chart. "On the seaward side."

All they could make out in the fast lowering blackness was a line of stark cliffs rising steeply out of the sea along the entire seaward side of the island.

"Jumping catfish, I don't see any sign of a landing," called Carl from the bow. "Shall I throw a sounding line?"

He did so without waiting for a reply and yelled back at once.

"Getting shallow, Bill. Slow her down."

Bill cut the engine throttle and at another cry from his brother brought the junk sharply around, yelling for bow and stern anchors to be heaved overboard.

The three companions stood in the stern, peering at the forbidding anchorage. Each of them was fully armed now with a pistol. A half-dozen of the rifles were stacked on deck and in the wheelhouse.

Bill studied their faces in the light of the stern lamp. He wondered just what they were thinking and if they were as scared as he was.

He said, "No sense trying to get ashore until morning. Let's set watches and take off in the dinghy early."

"Okay," was all his brother said. "Same as last night. I'll take the first if it's all right with Kats."

"Sure," Kats replied. "If there's any trouble, fire your gun."

Bill fell asleep exhausted in the dry, warm cabin the moment he stretched on the floor mats.

It seemed to him he had been asleep only a few seconds—it was actually almost four hours—when he heard the shouts of strange voices and the banging of a pistol outside.

He grabbed his own weapon which he had taken off and ran out the cabin door.

"Carl, Kats, what is it!"

Yells from his two companions came from the stern where in the dim light he saw them struggling

110

with a half-dozen men who were leaping aboard from a launch, dragging Carl and Kats back.

"Bill, help! help!" was all he heard before he saw them both go down.

He was afraid to shoot his pistol, fearing he might hit Carl or Kats. He charged along deck into the melee, swinging his gun like a club left and right at the boarders whom he now could see were roughly dressed Japanese fishermen or seamen.

He saw Carl and Kats being disarmed and caught, one bearded, squat fellow on the ear with his pistol butt before a terrible blow from a heavy club struck him on the back of the head and he went down, remembering as his last fleeting impression before losing consciousness the reeling of the stern lantern above him on its stubby mast and the continued cry for help from his brother, Carl.

The first moments of consciousness made Bill Maxwell aware that he was lying on his back with a throbbing head. He opened his eyes and made out above him what appeared to be the damp earthen roof of a cave.

The next moment, when he turned his head in the dim light, he caught the sound of familiar voices whispering—Kats, and Carl, and Dr. Sato! —and then he felt cool hands on his head and the welcome, although dirty and unshaven, face of his father was above him.

"Dad, thank heavens! What are you . . . where are we, anyway?"

His father placed a hand over Bill's lips.

"Not so loud, Bill. How's your head? We were pretty worried about you."

Bill reached up to feel the tender flesh at the back of his head and found a thick bandage there.

"Ouch, my head," he said as he tried to sit up. "Are you guys all right?"

"Yeah," Carl grinned nervously. "I sure didn't do a very good job of repelling boarders last night, though."

"Smugglers, you mean," said Kats.

Bill said his father look grimly across at Dr. Sato.

"So we were right. You did run into smugglers."

Bill groaned and lay back down, his head throbbing painfully.

"I'll say they did," Kats replied. "They got kidnapped right off Arako Island and . . ."

Bill's head felt clearer now that he was horizontal.

"Hey, wait," he said.

His father again motioned for him not to talk so loudly.

"Wait, you guys forget I haven't been around to hear about it. How about starting at the beginning."

It was Dr. Sato, in his quiet, unaccented voice who spoke.

"You remember I warned you about telling of our destination on our expedition?"

"Yes."

"Captain Tanaka of the Coast Guard warned us there was a great hunt on for opium smugglers in the locality of these islands. At first he did not want us to go to Arako at all because he thought news of our expedition might scare the smugglers into hiding, just as they were hoping to close the net. Then he changed his mind, hoping that an innocent archaeological party might discover some clue as to the whereabouts of this smuggling operation. You see, while the Coast Guard has known for months the smugglers were operating from somewhere around here, they have never been able to discover exactly where their—how do you call it—hideouts are."

"We discovered that—if we didn't find anything else, didn't we, Kwanjiro?" Bill's father asked, using Dr. Sato's first name.

Kats continued excitedly.

"There is an underwater cave on Arako—that is, a cave covered by high tide—remember the cliffs we saw at high tide yesterday morning, Bill?"

"I sure do."

"Father and Dr. Maxwell found the opening to the cave on the seaward wall at low tide, only the day before we got back."

Bill stared at Kats and Carl incredulously.

"The station on the chart in the junk!"

"Right. The cave—like this one—leads into huge dry caverns and can be entered by boat when the tide is half in or out. They have natural beaches in them where a boat can be drawn up. These are the hide-outs of this opium gang the Coast Guard has been searching for."

His father broke in.

"So we didn't discover any Tanshiro remains—but we did discover a cache of raw opium—and brought some back to camp. The scoundrels evidently observed us from hiding in the cave. At night they attacked us while we were asleep, threw us on their launch, and brought us here."

Bill sat up, feeling suddenly like laughing as the preposterous coincidence of the crewless junk became clear.

"Have you told Father how we got here?"

"Of course," said Carl.

"The splendid motor junk we thought was ours is now safely back in the smugglers' hide-out."

"As we are," added Bill's father, "although I don't know how safely."

Bill got unsteadily to his feet, looking toward the light in the mouth of the cave. The rays of sun, reflected on the ripples of the sea at the entrance, lighted the cave for two hundred feet. Beyond them, in the cavernous interior, lights and the figures of their captors were visible.

One of the two swarthy smugglers left to guard them—a short fellow armed with the very pistol Bill had worn the night before—moved to where Dr. Sato was sitting, and Bill heard them talking Japanese.

When the guard had retreated, Dr. Sato said, "He wants to know if we want something to eat."

Dr. Maxwell replied skeptically. "They're getting generous all at once. Tell him we do. We've got to try to keep up our strength."

Bill peered into the semi-darkness to the right of

the cave entrance where the smooth rise of the cave's underground beach could be partly distinguished.

"Is that where they keep the boats?"

"They've got a couple of fast launches—and of course the motor junk you delivered," his father said.

Bill sat down as Dr. Sato moved closer to him.

"Captain Tanaka would be most happy to get his hands on that 'pleasure' junk, as you boys call it, I'm sure. For months he has been looking for a link between the operators of the opium ring in Yokohama and the smugglers here. That boat— which looks like an innocent businessman's craft —is the link, I'm sure."

"You mean you think it belongs to whomever in Yokohama runs this gang?" asked Kats.

"Yes—I do."

"Then—he must be here."

Bill saw Dr. Sato nod in the affirmative as he interrupted to ask if Dr. Sato and his father had been told about the message left on Arako for the Coast Guard.

"Yes, of course they told us," Bill's father said. "But we can't be sure they'll see it for days in this typhoon weather."

Their guard had returned, with a third Japanese seaman who carried a tray on which was a kettle of soggy rice and a pan of half-burned fried fish.

They turned as Dr. Sato motioned silently in the direction of the lanterns at the far underground reach of the cavern. They heard the sound of voices rising in loud jest suddenly. Their two guards and the man who had brought the food had gone back to join the dozen others.

Kats said, "Did you hear what that short fellow with the beard said, Father?"

"Yes, I heard."

"What was it?" asked Bill.

"He was joking about our bringing the junk back to them."

They listened to the rising clamor of drunken laughter coming from the cave.

Dr. Sato's small face twisted in a pained expression as he turned to Bill's father.

"They may be joking now, but our position here is not a joking matter, believe me, Walter. I know this kind of men. They are savage, heedless of human life. They will do anything to make a few yen."

He wiped his hands on his trousers and went on.

"From scraps of conversation yesterday I gather they intended to go off and leave us. They have another hide-out near Chejo Island off the south coast of Korea. But get them full of sake—which appears to be the situation now—" He paused to listen to the drunken brawling—"and there is no saying what they will do."

Bill stared at Carl and Kats, thinking again of the powerful junk which lay within a few seconds' hard run down the sand beach near the cave's mouth.

"Father, Dr. Sato."

He shifted to be closer to the two men.

"Here's our chance. The three of us know everything about that junk!"

116

He saw Kats and Carl nodding in agreement.

"We could get it going in a matter of seconds."

His father shook his head, running his hand over his scraggly beard.

"It's too great a risk, Bill. They'd be after us in a minute—and they're armed, don't forget."

The four of them looked at Dr. Sato, who raised himself from his squatting position to study the beach.

"I believe, Walter, the risk is worth taking. If the boys can get that boat started, we can at least defend ourselves better on the boat than we can here."

Dr. Maxwell peered at the back of the cave where the smugglers—as noisy as before—were gathered around a charcoal fire at a distance of about a hundred feet.

"All right." Bill saw his father tense and gather his legs under him.

"I'm ready if you are, Bill; you and I will run in the lead. If there are guards by the boats, try a tackle so the others can get to the junk."

Bill felt his head pulse achingly as he dug his feet into the sand.

His father looked around, then tapped his arm. "Ready, Carl, Kats—come on, let's go!"

They ran noiselessly over the edge of the beach and down the sharply sloping, hard sand. There was not a guard in sight. A few seconds splashing in the water and Bill and his father were clambering up the boarding ladder on the stern of the junk, then reaching down to pull Kats, Carl, and Dr. Sato aboard.

"Check the engine, Kats!" Bill hissed as he ran for the wheelhouse.

"Carl, you get the stern line off!"

He dashed into the wheelhouse, seeing his father was already in the bow tugging to loosen the anchor line there. He pushed the starter switch at the same time advancing the full-ahead lever, feeling a surge of triumph as the engine throbbed into life. He spun the wheel to port, heading the boat toward the semi-circle of daylight which marked the cave's entrance.

At the same instant he heard a chorus of hoarse cries at the back of the cave and over his shoulder saw the entire gang of smugglers jump to their feet.

In a moment the junk's mast had cleared the cave's mouth and the brilliant sunlight burst over them as they sailed into the sea outside.

Kats came running up the engine room stairs.

"Atta boy, Bill, we made it!"

There was a reassuring yell from Carl, and then his father and Dr. Sato entered the wheelhouse.

"They'll be after us in a minute," his father said, breathing hard.

"How fast will this boat go?"

Bill headed the junk toward the point at the northern end of the island.

"Not fast enough to keep ahead of those launches. Better see if they left any of the guns aboard. Kats knows where they are."

When he looked astern, as they neared the island's north promontory, Bill saw first one, then the second black painted launch emerge from the cave's entrance and turn to speed after them, their sharp bows throwing up furrows of white foam.

Kats came running back.

"Not a single gun aboard, Bill."

Bill remembered the dinghy.

"Get the dinghy oars, Kats, and—anything to use for throwing. Canned stuff in the cabin—anything you can think of."

The launches following were gaining. When he glanced astern the third time he saw a man in the bow of the lead launch raise a rifle and a split second later a bullet smashed out a window in the wheelhouse, sending a shower of glass over the wheel.

They were at the point.

Bill spun the wheel to send them around it as close to the rocks as he dared, hoping for a few minutes protection the cliff would give.

He saw his father and Dr. Sato in the stern, each with a dinghy oar prepared to repel boarders as best they could. He ducked automatically as a hail of bullets crashed into the side of the wheelhouse.

The next instant there was a yell of astonishment from his brother. Before Bill could take his eyes from the launch—almost abreast of them—the echoing boom of a ship's gun sounded off the cliff, and a giant geyser of water shot up at the launch's bow, literally throwing the speeding boat up and away so that it was nearly capsized and almost filled with water.

Bill swung around to face the bow, thinking he must be seeing a mirage.

A quarter of a mile away he saw the long, sleek white hull of a Coast Guard ship, its guns and superstructure gleaming in the sunlight.

At the same second he heard the report of a bow gun and another shell whistled over the wheelhouse, landing so close to the second launch it was instantly capsized and the men aboard all thrown into the water.

Dr. Sato and Bill's father had dropped their oars and rushed to the bow of the junk, while Kats and Carl stood waving and shouting.

In five minutes the Coast Guard ship—Bill could see the *Osaka Maru* plainly now—was alongside. From the bridge a stout, red-faced man in a white uniform was waving and calling in Japanese to Dr. Sato.

One of the ship's launches appeared then, speeding from the opposite side to the spot where the two smugglers' boats with their crews lay helpless in the water.

The big Coast Guard ship was nearly into port at Yokohama—later that afternoon—before all of them were gathered in the officers mess for tea and a recounting of the past days' events.

They had seen the smugglers' boats lifted aboard with the ship's davits and the junk taken in tow. The excitement was over.

120

Captain Tanaka, jolly and talkative, and his first mate, plied them with questions, with Dr. Sato doing the translating and Kats interrupting frequently with his own version.

"I found your message, of course. As you guessed," Captain Tanaka was saying, "we were kept busy for three days assisting the fishing vessels all over the bay—there were nearly a dozen lost—and did not patrol by Arako until this morning. We went ashore at once."

Dr. Maxwell was helping himself to another cup of tea and more wafers.

"Nothing has ever looked as good as the sight of your ship off Konshu, Captain. I must confess"—he glanced at his colleague—"I felt like a fool standing there on that junk waiting to fight off those armed smugglers with rowboat oars."

"Dinghy oars, Father," Carl corrected.

Bill broke in with the question uppermost in the concern of three of them.

"What about that junk, Captain Tanaka? Did you find the owner?"

The captain slapped the table with a heavy fist when Dr. Sato had translated the question.

"The owner of the vessel is not among the smugglers, but we have the registration papers. The information in them will be of great interest to the Narcotics Bureau of the government, I can assure you. It belongs to a certain merchant in Yokohama we have long suspected was involved in this dirty business."

121

"Is it true you have a right to keep a boat if you find it without a crew at sea?" asked Bill.

The Captain grinned and folded his hands across his stomach, speaking to Dr. Sato so he could translate.

"The maritime law applies to wrecked or sunken vessels, generally, not ships that have slipped their moorings. However—" he winked slyly at Dr. Maxwell—"the junk will come now under the classification of confiscated goods, and in that case I think you may assume that with the right word in the right places the boat is as good as yours."

"Did you hear that!" Kats jumped to his feet, unable to restrain himself.

"We get to keep the ghost junk!"

The captain added thoughtfully.

"After all, it is to you"—he bowed to the two archaeologists—"and you three fine sailors that the Coast Guard owes the discovery of this hideout which has caused us months of search."

Bill got up. His brother and Kats joined him, guessing his destination.

"Mind if we go take a look at how she's riding on the towrope?"

His father studied the three of them standing there, the expression of pride on his face evident to everyone in the room.

"Go along and see your boat, fellows."

He got up, his tea cup in his hand as if to offer a toast.

"And since your boat will need a name, I would like to propose one."

122

He indicated his diminutive colleague.

"I propose the boat be named for one of Japan's finest scholars, who is also a gentleman of great courage—Dr. Kwanjiro Sato. And . . ." he added . . . "for his son, a good sailor. Gentlemen, I give you—the *Sato Maru.*"

The Haunted Pavilion

◆━━◆━━◆━━◆━━◆

PATRICIA MC CUNE

VICKIE HAMILTON jerked off the summer blanket and pulled herself to a half sitting position against the rumpled pillow. The night was still dark, filtered gray with thin fog. But no sense in trying to sleep, she thought, the afternoon's anger departing from her slowly.

"Imagine that director of the 'Little Theater by the Sea'—that Mr. Forbes—saying I was too young to have any part," she'd complained before dinner to Jay Bourke. "Why, I'm practically eighteen and I'll be out of school in a few more weeks. Besides, I've been interested in acting all my life!"

"Yeah, you'd think they'd always need someone to be a maid, or a page, or part of a crowd, or even a seventeen-year-old." Jay had grinned then, his eyes blue spears of laughter, and Vickie had forgotten her irritation for a moment. Jay Bourke had made moving to Forbes Bay a pleasant thing, until the director of the "Little Theater by the Sea" spoiled everything with his silly rules. Mr. Forbes was also the mayor, and the owner of Forbes Boats, and those same rules hadn't kept his daughter, Kate, from trying out for a part in the new production, Vickie noticed.

Vickie had been so careful during the tryouts. She read the play in advance a half-dozen times in order to understand it and the significance of each role. And on the stage, before she began reading, she waited a long time to get the proper feeling of the character. Then she read slowly. Kept the script away from her face. Didn't slur her words. She paid close attention to projecting her voice and emphasising correctly.

And nobody could say she was an outsider, not interested in the history of "The Little Theater by the Sea" and other landmarks of Forbes Bay. Before the tryouts, she wandered through the abandoned and deteriorating pavilion and couldn't help asking about it after the readings had been completed.

"Mr. Forbes, you're the mayor, aren't you?"

He nodded his narrow, balding head and Vickie noticed his eyes looked pinched and guarded.

"Maybe you know why the pavilion is so deserted. It seems a fascinating place to me, but when I searched it earlier there wasn't a soul around."

Mr. Forbes seemed suddenly interested, answering quickly, and moving closer to Vickie. "I'm sure it isn't as deserted as you say. Or do you go there often?"

"No. I live on the other side of the bay. I came

over today for the reading. I like to explore and since I got here early, the pavilion seemed a good place for it."

"You live on the other side of the bay?" Mr. Forbes asked intently and hunched his bony shoulders over Vickie so closely she was sorry she had talked to him at all. "Do you have a boat? How did you get here?"

"Well, my mother drove me around the highway. She's going to pick me up in a few minutes. Can you tell me if I got the part, Mr. Forbes? Was I all right?"

Mr. Forbes turned his head and didn't answer immediately. Vickie didn't want to disturb him if he was thinking about it, but he seemed ages answering her.

"Mr. Forbes?"

"Well, Vickie," he began, and his tight little eyes expanded in their intensity, "I think you did a fair job, but it was not quite as well handled as I think it should be."

"I can read for another part, Mr. Forbes. Please."

"I'm afraid you're too young. You need a few more years of growing up. We have rules governing age here, you see."

Vickie's mouth flew open in protest, but she could not speak. She watched him turn his back and walk away, and her anger began to boil inside her.

Now she flopped against the pillow and examined the luminous clock on the bedside table, anger renewing with each fresh thought that tumbled one after the other through her mind. It was two-thirty in the middle of the night and she hated Mr. Forbes with daytime energy, and grabbed her robe and slippers and flew from her bed.

Vickie made three circles in haste around the room, settling finally by the window at the foot of her bed, where she often sat in the early morning as light glided in over the roof tops, or at the edge of evening, when the pavilion across the bay stood dark against the blushing sky. Now there was nothing in the night to see. She pressed closer to the window to sharpen her vision and brushed the curtains across the pane as if to clear the wispy fog away.

Then stealthily, without prelude, something nebulous and filmy slipped into the pavilion landing. A boat. It would have to be a boat.

"My gosh." Vickie tugged at the window until it was opened wide, then pushed her face against the screen. "Maybe it's a fishing boat taking on some fishermen," she whispered to herself knowing it wasn't true. In another hour or so, fishing boats would chug down the bay to the ocean, but they would hold a course straight and sure down the main channel, the dull, explosive sounds of their engines muted but unmistakable in the fog.

Whatever kind of boat it was, barely visible now at the pavilion dock, it had purposely sneaked in under the fog's cover. No sound of engines echoed across the bay. No warning bark of fog horn. There were no running lights.

Vickie watched in speechless fascination as the

128

ghost ship disgorged two shrouded figures who floated up the ramp and into the recesses of the pavilion like two white phantoms sucked into an unknown blackness.

"My gosh," Vickie repeated, aching to call her mother in the next room, and at the same time attached to the window like a golden moth to a burst of light.

In a moment the boat, blanketed in night mist, eased away from the pavilion and disappeared. "But it was there," Vickie said, "I saw it."

In the morning, Vickie discovered no one else had been immobile or spellbound beside an open window. No one else had seen two white figures emerge from the boat at the pavilion dock.

"No," Mrs. Hamilton said. "You must have been dreaming, Vickie. Or dramatizing. Why didn't you call me?"

"I guess it all happened too fast. But Mother, I wasn't dreaming."

When Vickie told her story a second time, on the sand, Jay Bourke turned serious for an instant, then lost his words in hasty laughter. "Didn't you know we had a haunted pavilion, Vickie?"

"Be serious, Jay."

"I am."

"Well, tell me what you mean then."

"I mean you're not the only one who's seen the ghosts."

"I didn't call them ghosts."

"Well, other people have. You might as well.

129

I've never seen them, but everyone believes our pavilion is haunted."

Vickie caught the trace of amusement that threaded through his solemn announcement and wondered whether to pursue her questioning or b'de her time. She and her mother had lived in ⁻orbes Bay only a few months. Maybe it was better not to move too fast into the supersititions of the natives.

Her curiosity, imprisoned momentarily by caution, was about to slip through the web again, when ⁻ate Forbes appeared suddenly and dropped to ⁻he sand beside Jay.

"Hi." Kate's dark eyes shone against her tanned skin and short black hair, and without thinking Vickie pushed her own blond bangs back from her forehead. Small twists of warmth pressed through her, the same hate she'd felt last night for Mr. Forbes, transferring now to his daughter, Kate, and a new jealousy for Kate alone, undefined, but centered definitely in Jay Bourke. Tall, muscular Jay, who could row a boat swiftly and swim like a porpoise, and who dated Kate regularly before Vickie moved to Forbes Bay.

Vickie looked up and said, "Hi," and tried to hide her feelings.

"Vickie saw the ghosts last night," Jay said with the mixture of laughter and seriousness he had in his voice before.

"Did you—really?" Kate spoke hesitantly, with a strange effort Vickie didn't understand.

"I don't exactly believe in ghosts, but I saw—"

130

Vickie stopped quickly when a streak of fear crossed Kate's face, and a silence pulled at them all until Kate laughed abruptly.

"Remember when we tried to see the ghosts, Jay?" Kate asked.

"Yeah." Jay shook his head and Vickie's curiosity was back again, full force.

"Oh, tell me."

"We stayed up all night," Jay said.

"Three different nights," Kate added, the fear brooding over her face. "A whole gang of us."

"But you never saw them?"

"No," Jay said, disgusted. "These ghosts first appeared about three years ago, and for six months off and on I tried every way I knew to see them. Never did. And you, Vickie, after a couple of months at Forbes Bay, saunter over to your window, glance across the bay, and there they are. No justice." His sudden smile lightened the mood again. Ghosts began to seem unreal in the brightness of hard blue sky, reflecting water, and burning sand. Vickie's mind jumped back to the "Little Theater by the Sea."

"Kate, tell me why your father won't let me have a part in the new play." The question had turned over many times in Vickie's own thoughts, but Kate was startled by it, unprepared.

"Why—I—"

"Will you take me over to the Little Theater, Kate, and let me walk out on the empty stage one last time? Let me say a few words of dialogue. I

131

have things memorized. Let me make an entrance and pretend—"

"I can't, Vickie. I just can't." Kate stood up and brushed the sand from her bathing suit and backed away from Vickie. "My father wouldn't like it. I don't know why. I wouldn't mind taking you, but —I'll see you later. I've got to go now."

Vickie watched Kate walk across the sand and climb over the low sea wall and move on down the boardwalk. She saw that Jay was watching, too, and neither said a word for a long time, but felt the sun on their backs and a fresh breeze beginning to stir.

"Jay?" Vickie sat up finally and gazed across the bay.

"Yes?"

"Take me over to the pavilion. Please. We can row over in your rowboat. Will you?"

"For a minute I thought you'd forgotten the ghosts."

"For a minute I had."

"They won't be there now, Vickie. Whatever you saw last night is long gone."

"I know. I just want to see the pavilion again. And look around. I should think you'd be curious, too."

"Vickie, I told you I spent hours and days and weeks and months being curious. Those ghosts are —well—ghosts. They don't show up every night, you know. They might not come back again for six months."

"Jay, we know that mystery boat won't ever
132

come in when the night is clear. It's the foggy, misty, moonless nights we should watch. Like last night. Well, isn't that right?"

"I guess so."

Vickie looked at him closely and he turned his head under her scrutiny. "There's something you're not telling me, Jay Bourke. What is it? Come on now."

Jay shrugged and looked at Vickie and finally smiled. "I guess I might as well tell you. Nobody else ever saw a boat. Different people swore they saw the ghosts, but no one ever saw a boat. Only you."

"I saw it, Jay. I know I did."

"But don't you understand that before, when we waited to see the ghosts, the nights were clear. Sometimes the moon lit up half the bay." Jay tightened his lips. "Wouldn't you know we'd do something stupid like that? 'Course we were real kids then. Three years ago. The only night it was the slightest bit cloudy was one Halloween. And everyone in Forbes Bay was dressed up like a ghost. Nobody understands what's going on so once a year they make a joke of it. The rest of the time they ignore it. But there's sure only one kind of Halloween costume in this town."

Vickie laughed. "So now all we have to do is watch the weather, and steer clear of Halloween."

"Summer's coming on. We may have a long wait for the right weather."

"That's why I want to see the pavilion again.

133

Maybe you've seen it a thousand times, but remember I've only been at Forbes Bay a little while."

"Well, okay. Come on."

With long easy strokes, Jay rowed to the peninsula side of the bay, Vickie sitting in the stern of the rowboat, the gray pavilion looming larger as they neared, its dome piercing the sky.

"Is there anything up in that dome, Jay?"

"Used to be a dance hall before the ghosts got it."

Vickie could see the windows that circled the dome high above the water. Probably where the dancing couples gazed down at the rippling currents of the bay while the soft music played around them, she thought.

"Do you want to pull up on the sand, or tie up at the pavilion dock?" Jay asked.

"Well, I'm not afraid, if that's what you mean," Vickie answered. "Don't boats use the landing any more?"

"Nope. Used to be canoe rentals, motor boat rentals, sight-seeing boats. Anything you wanted. Now nothing." Jay brought the rowboat into one of the smaller pavilion slips and tied the painter while Vickie jumped out. She stood still for a moment on the dock looking around her at the deserted, creaking, three-level structure.

The ramp was steep in low tide and they climbed slowly to street level where a half dozen shops and stores gaped their emptiness on both sides of the open-air walk. Vickie read the weathered signs —fishing tackle—barber shop—ice cream—

"What on earth happened to everyone?" she asked.

"Well, if a place is haunted you'll hardly ever find people around. Come on upstairs. We'll have a look at the old dance hall. I used to hear the music floating across the bay when they danced on Saturday nights. And the view's good."

"Maybe that's where we should be the next night the fog is heavy."

"Might not be too bad an idea." Jay looked at Vickie closely. "Would you really come here at night?"

"Not alone."

"With me?"

Vickie nodded. She stood next to him by the wide circle of windows in the pavilion dome and without wanting to, thought of Kate Forbes. "Jay? Did you think Kate acted kind of strange?"

"Yes, I guess so."

"Was it because of—well, me? Or was it all about the Little Theater and Mr. Forbes?"

"Both."

"Do you think we could go to the Little Theater now that we're over here? I want to look at the stage and maybe walk out on it and—"

But Jay wasn't listening. He streaked across the dance floor to the far side of the room. There he grabbed something from the floor and ran back to Vickie with it. "A Halloween costume," he said, and Vickie knew all the joking had gone out of him. She held her breath without speaking. Questions churned

135

in her mind and she wondered a hundred things at once.

"There's a label in it, Vickie. This is no home-made ghost costume." He read carefully. "Property of 'Little Theater by the Sea' Wardrobe Department." He stared at her with his deep-blue eyes and after a long silence spoke again. "They rent costumes when there's any occasion to rent them. We needn't jump to any conclusions."

"That Mr. Forbes. That hateful Mr. Forbes. No wonder he asked me where I lived and if I had a boat and if I visited the pavilion often. But why should he get himself mixed up with a haunted pavilion and ghosts that aren't really ghosts?"

"I said we'd better not jump to any conclusions."

"Well, it's probably why he didn't want me in his play. Coming across the bay every day. Exploring around where maybe I shouldn't. He was afraid I might discover something he didn't want me to discover."

"Yes, but what is it we've discovered?" Jay rubbed his hand across the top of his bristly sun-bleached hair. "We found a ghost costume up here in the old dance hall. What does that prove?"

"It certainly proves the ghost who was wearing that costume got out of it and accidentally left it here."

"But why, Vickie, why? And why do you think Mr. Forbes has anything to do with it just because of a label?"

"In the first place, he's the only one in Forbes

136

Bay who isn't friendly and he practically owns the town."

"That's no reason."

"And in the second place, Kate started acting strange the minute I asked about her father and mentioned seeing the ghosts."

"She just might be acting strange because I spend so much time with you, you know." He smiled a little crooked smile, but Vickie was too absorbed to notice.

"She wouldn't have waited until today to show her feelings. And in the third place, who could rig up a boat so it wouldn't make a sound yet would still move, except the owner of a boat company? Forbes Boats, remember? And all those questions he asked me. Jay, do you think Kate knows something or do you think she suspects?"

"Vickie, you get so dramatic, I'm sure you'll be a great actress some day. We're miles ahead of ourselves. Slow down."

Jay took her hand and pulled her down the pavilion steps to the open-air walk, past the empty shops to the ramp. He didn't speak until she was safely in the rowboat and he'd rowed halfway across the bay. "There might be fog again tonight," he said finally.

"Jay, do you think we should go to the police?"

Jay took a deep breath and yanked on the oars. "We have three policemen in this little town. I think if we went to them they'd go straight to Mr. Forbes."

"You believe me then? You agree with me about

Mr. Forbes? You think I'm right about the ghosts? You do, I know you do." The words tumbled out of her mouth so fast, one after the other, that Jay laughed.

"I'd love to see you on the stage, Vickie."

"I know one thing, Jay Bourke. Half the time when you're laughing you should be serious."

"I am serious. I think the police must be part of Mr. Forbes' plan. Else why haven't they tried to do something? Of course maybe they have and we don't know about it."

"Just what do you suppose Mr. Forbes' plan is?"

"Well, I'd say if we could capture ourselves a couple of ghosts some foggy night, maybe we'd find out what the scheme is."

"Jay, do you think we could do it? Alone? I mean together? The two of us?"

"Well, I don't think anyone else would believe our story right now, do you?" He laughed again and Vickie laughed with him.

"Not even my own mother," she said.

June was a foggy month. Each day the sun burned all morning before the last remnant of night mist disappeared. Each evening the fog bank pressed in over the ocean, filtered through the trees and over the buildings, crawling its way across Forbes Bay, disguising landmarks as it spread.

Vickie received Jay's telephone call at ten-fifteen one June night three weeks after their careful plans had been completed. "You ready?" His whisper was ominous.

"My gosh, Jay, you mean tonight? So soon?" Little jabs of excitement raced through her.

"I hope I mean tonight. I could be wrong. Mr. Forbes left his house about—"

"Talk louder, Jay. I can't hear you."

"Well, I don't want the whole world to hear. I said he left his house about nine forty-five, went straight to his own dock, hopped into one of his motor boats, and took off into the fog."

"My gosh."

"Vickie, where's your mom? What are you going to tell her?"

"She's down the street playing cards now. I'll leave her a note that I've gone out with you. But she'll worry if I'm late."

"You know we'll be late. You'll have to tell her we'll be very late. Vickie, I'll be there in five minutes."

Vickie hung up the telephone, grabbed a jacket and scarf, and from the floor of her closet, a brown paper sack. By the time she'd finished the note to her mother, Jay was running up the front walk. She felt wonderfully dramatic and scared at the same time.

Secretly, Jay had watched the Forbes house for three weeks, waiting for Mr. Forbes to make a move that would seem unusual or unexpected. They'd thought of the idea when the fog became consistently heavy at night.

"Come on." Jay took her hand and they moved

noiselessly through the heavy mist to the rowboat. "We probably have hours to wait, but I'd rather wait on the other side of the bay."

"Got the flashlight?"

"Yeah, did you bring the sheets?"

"You mean our costumes. In here." She lifted the brown paper sack. "How about dimes for the telephone?"

"Got them. Here, you should keep them. And I have the rope. Are you scared, Vickie?"

"Well, a little, I guess." Still she had to admit that wearing a costume and acting out this part came closer to being in a play than anything else she'd done here. Of course, the audience was missing.

"Here we are." Jay helped Vickie over the sea wall and together they crossed the short strip of sand to the rowboat. "Hop in."

Jay untied the painter from the mooring line and shoved the rowboat out into the bay, and Vickie could hear the scrape of sand against the bottom of the boat. She could hear Jay pull up the oar locks and place the oars in them, and the muted splash as the oars hit the water. With each stroke, she could hear the leather binding grind against the metal locks, and the toneless dip, dip, dip of the oars into the water.

She could feel the mist clinging to her face, wet and cool. She could feel the tide draw. The pulse of the current. She could feel the black night. Unfamiliar, unaccountable, exciting.

But she couldn't see. The quarter-moon had been

long hidden. There were no stars. Lights in the houses had blinked out as the night advanced. It seemed hours before they crossed the bay and touched sand again.

"We're off course," Jay said, and Vickie knew in the dense fog they'd landed much farther from the pavilion than they'd planned.

"What'll we do?"

"We'll have to drift down closer," Jay said. "We don't dare get too far away from this boat. Just in case." He smiled, and Vickie clutched the brown paper bag and tried to smile back as they moved on down the bay.

"It'll be warmer and drier up in the dance hall, don't you think?" Vickie shivered in a sudden flurry of cold air.

"But first we'll have to throw on our sheets—"

"—costumes."

"We'll have to put them on here. It's pretty late and pretty lousy weather for midnight strollers, but if anyone sees us, we don't want them knowing who we are just yet."

After they secured the boat, Vickie opened the sack and handed Jay a sheet, and threw one over her head and shoulders, wrapping it around her in the way she'd practiced at home. She pinned it in several places and then helped Jay with his.

"Ready?" Jay asked. "We'll walk in the sand to the pavilion, go in the street entrance and straight up the stairs." Jay took her hand and led her slowly to the pavilion. And her heart thumped wildly with each cautious step.

"How do we know the mystery boat hasn't already arrived? Don't you think we'd better check the landing before we go upstairs?" Vickie asked, holding his hand tightly.

"We're early. You know we're early."

"Who says the ghosts have to come at the same time they did before? It's foggier tonight than it was the night I saw them. If I were looking out my window right now, I couldn't see one thing across the bay."

"Okay. I'll sneak down the ramp and have a look. You can wait for me."

"Oh, no you don't, Jay Bourke. You don't leave me. That wasn't part of our plan. I'm going with you."

"All right. But remember no talking." He stopped for a moment in the open-air walk and leaned down to her face to see her eyes. "Vickie, we can still go home if you're scared."

"I'm scared all right, but we're not going home."

So with hands clutching, they eased down the ramp of the pavilion dock. They could see only a few feet ahead of them and strained their ears for sounds, familiar or not. Any sound. All sounds. They heard the creaking of the flat. The swish of the current around the pilings. Otherwise a deafening silence throbbed in their ears.

Then Jay's hand tightened over hers. Faint dronings of an electric motor reached them. Lapping of a bow wave. Vickie suddenly wanted to scream, to run, to hide. She was frozen in a moment of panic as the bow of the mystery boat sliced the water, and in a slow deliberate motion reversed to dock. She knew she and Jay would have to get off the ramp in a matter of seconds. She knew they'd never make it to the dance hall steps.

Her legs were stiff and immovable. She felt Jay's arm across her shoulder and tried to breathe again. Swiftly he pulled her up the ramp and shoved her against the wall of the empty fishing tackle shop and clamped his hand over her mouth until her shoulders sagged in relaxation. He looked closely into her face and finally she nodded her head and he nodded back and returned to the entrance of the shop to wait.

In a few seconds the first ghost floated up the ramp past the fishing tackle shop and out the open-air walk to the street, not looking back into the thick fog; not knowing that Jay had stepped out into the walk before the unsuspecting second ghost appeared. In costume, it was not difficult for Jay to waylay the trusting follower and beckon him into the fishing tackle shop. With quick, strong, surprise movements, Jay downed the ghost and, Vickie helping, bound him securely.

Hurriedly, they ran out the open-air walk, Vickie to the public telephone on the corner, Jay to the "Little Theater by the Sea," a block and a half off the main street.

"You wait right there until you see a patrol car," Jay called over his shoulder, the first either had spoken in ages. His voice sounded wonderful.

"Be careful," she called through the partially opened door of the booth, ready to dial the numbers she'd memorized. Four calls. The Forbes Bay Police. Harbor Master. State Police. County Sheriff.

"Just in case," Jay said when they made their plans earlier. "I don't mind catching the ghosts, but I sure won't know what to do with them after I get them." They laughed then, but telephoning now, Vickie knew she wouldn't laugh until it was all over safely.

She reached for the first dime under the folds of the sheet, but in her excitement missed the telephone coin slot and with a sickening feeling heard the dime clink against the telephone, drop to the ground and roll out of reach in a crack outside the door she hadn't fully closed. "Darn," she said angrily. "First I freeze and Jay has to drag me up the ramp and now I delay everything by losing a dime."

She grabbed for the other coins, glad she'd brought extras, but her pocket was empty. The dimes were not there. Gone.

"But they have to be here. I put them in my pocket, myself."

She felt more carefully and her finger slipped through a tiny hole in the pocket. In an overwhelming moment of panic, she knew she'd lost the money. But the dime in the crack. She'd get it out somehow. She could reach the telephone operator with one dime. She opened the door and as the light went out in the telephone booth, a filmy specter floated around the corner in the fog, and Vickie fell to her knees against the telephone booth as the apparition wafted past her. "My gosh," she moaned. "Our ghost! Our tied-up ghost! He escaped from the fishing tackle shop. He got himself loose!"

She thought of Jay battling two ghosts at the Little Theater and in sudden terror wondered if they could have been wrong about Mr. Forbes. They'd been wrong about the time. Wrong about the ghosts going to the dance hall. But they just couldn't be wrong about Mr. Forbes.

She labored frantically in the dark to pull the thin coin from the narrow crack where it had lodged. She had to get it out. Maybe Jay's life depended on it. When it finally came loose in her hand, she almost cried with relief, and gripped it tightly until it was released safely down the coin slot and she could give the operator her four calls.

The police cars would have to use the highway, driving the long way around the bay and down the peninsula, unless they were patrolling nearby. But it didn't really take long although it seemed forever. Vickie had promised Jay not to follow him after she completed the telephone calls, so to hurry the time, she removed her sheet, folded it, and pushed it under her arm.

When the first patrol car pulled up silently without the siren, Vickie stepped into the gutter where she might be seen in the flare of the fog lights. The patrol car stopped and she jumped in.

When they arrived at the Little Theater, Jay was standing on the stage, and Mr. Forbes, still wearing his ghost costume, was sitting in one of the front-row setas, his hands tied. And lashed to the seat next to him was the second ghost.

"Vickie, you all right?" Jay jumped down from the stage and ran to her as the police and the newly arrived harbor master took over the ghosts. "Say, how'd that guy get loose, anyway? He sure surprised me. But he was so mad at Mr. Forbes for letting him get caught, that I got almost the whole story."

"Well, tell me."

"You won't believe it, but he was bringing people into this country illegally."

"He was what?"

"You know. Illegal entry. From Mexico. People from all countries who aren't allowed in our country for one reason or another. And he did it all for a nice fat chunk of money."

"Jay, I know he couldn't have gone all the way down to Mexico."

"Of course not. His boat, which has that electric auxiliary motor, remember, would meet another boat at a prearranged place out in the ocean."

"In this fog?"

"Well, that's what they'd do. And they'd transfer the passenger. Mr. Forbes only brought in one at a time. Then the guy would stay in the Little Theater until daylight and hop a bus for the big city the next morning. No one in Forbes Bay was the wiser. Until you came along, of course."

"He told you all that?"

"I got most of it from the angry foreigner. Speaks good English. Mr. Forbes shut up. Said he wanted to see his lawyer."

"But why all the ghosts? Nobody'd probably ever see them if they wore dark suits."

"Don't you see he had to clear out the pavilion. It wasn't bringing him in much money any more, and he couldn't take chances with people around. So he haunted it." The old lightness was back in Jay's voice and Vickie smiled. It was only the thought of Kate Forbes that sobered her. There was no hate now for Kate; no jealousy. Just pity.

"What's poor Kate going to do? Did she know about her father?"

"Mr. Forbes' family probably didn't know. I think Kate must have been suspicious. She'll be all right. We'll help her."

Within a few minutes the police had taken over in full force. Even the Forbes Bay police were astonished. "Hey, kids, you did all right," one of the patrolmen called. "How'd you ever figure this one out?"

Vickie and Jay grinned and another policeman slapped Jay on the back. "Want a ride home?"

"No thanks. Got my rowboat."

"Well, there's nothing more for you to do here tonight. We'll get in touch with you in the morning. You better get along home."

Vickie and Jay were strangely silent on the way home. Tomorrow they would talk about the night's adventure, but now there was something satisfying in the quiet, damp and soft around them. When they did speak it was not of the ghosts.

"Did you see me up on the stage, Vickie?"

"Of course I did."

"How did I look—well, I mean, I think maybe when we get a new director for the Little Theater I'll audition with you."

Vickie leaned back in the boat and closed her eyes and tilted her head so the mist fell on her face with new freshness. It would be wonderful, she thought, without opening her eyes, if she and Jay could be in a play together when the "Little Theater by the Sea" found a new director.

"I'd like that, Jay," was all she said. And they rowed home peacefully through the foggy night.

The Haunted Tumbler

◆━◆━◆━◆━◆

DIANA MEYERS

SANDRA KELLY maneuvered her jalopy cautiously through the heavy downpour of the winter evening. She was thinking, "It's just like Tom to ask me to drive across town in this miserable weather, just to bring him something to eat. How did I ever get the job of errand-girl for those guys, anyhow?"

She was still fuming about how she was expected to cater to her three older brothers, when she stopped in front of an old brick building. Although Sandra thought the word "spooky" was childish, she had always thought of it in connection with the building, which was identified by the lettering on the front door, "WARREN'S DRY CLEANERS, Wholesale Only."

She ran through the rain to the iron gate, which closed off the driveway at the side of the building. She stood by the gate, huddling into her parka-coat to protect herself against the driving wet wind. She prayed silently, "Please, Tom, please come this way!"

Finally, she did see her brother coming down the driveway. He grinned when he saw her, the dimples in his smile making him seem younger than nineteen. "Why didn't you ring the buzzer? Look at you, you're sopping wet!"

He looked puzzled when she said, "I forgot about the buzzer." Sanda would rather fib to him than admit that she preferred getting drenched to touching the electric buzzer in the rain.

He took the lunch box she carried. "Thanks! You're a good kid, Sam!"

Sandra winced at the hated nickname, a leftover from her tomboy days, when she had tagged after her brothers. Since she had been in high school, she had abandoned her boyish ways. She longed to be as feminine as her brothers' girl friends. The only time the boys called her Sandra, however, was when they wanted to borrow her jalopy.

Now Tom winked at her wickedly. "Come on, Sam; *Greg* is in the back!" Sandra felt her face flush, even in the cold, wet air. She thought she had hidden her feelings about Greg Warren.

She and Tom ran down the driveway, which extended the entire length of the brick building. At the corner of the building, they turned left into a cement yard, covered by a galvanized roof. The driveway continued about twenty feet beyond the yardway, ending at the entrance to a shed.

The section of the driveway leading to the shed was also covered with a galvanized roof, and this dark passageway seemed to Sandra the most frightening place in the plant.

150

They walked across the yardway to another brick building, smaller than the front building, but still a large structure. Sandra knew this was the cleaning room, and it was the only plant building she had been in since Tom had started working with Greg Warren on the part-time night shift.

Greg was working in the cleaning room, and Sandra admired every movement of his tall, muscular body. Sandra thought her oldest brother, Patrick, was the most sophisticated man she knew; her brother, Kevin, one of the handsomest she'd ever seen; and Tom, the most ambitious and hard-working. She was sure, though, that Greg Warren far outstripped her brothers in all attributes. He was just about perfect, except for one flaw. He didn't seem to notice she was a girl.

Now she was giddy with excitement, as he strode toward her. "Am I glad you're here, Sam! Your brother couldn't concentrate on the cleaning, he was so worried about missing his supper!"

Tom laughed, "Sure, 'cause I think you made up that story about having to drive out to Peerless to pick up their load. I'm stuck here with cold sandwiches, and I'll bet you really have a hot date with some chick!"

"Well, if it's any consolation, my chick and I will be thinking of you and your sandwiches."

Sandra thought they were kidding, but she wasn't sure. She straightened her five feet seven inch frame and took a deep breath. She felt as though she were diving into a barrel of cleaning solvent, but she took the plunge. "You know, Greg, I've been here a couple of times, but I've never seen much of the plant. Are you awfully busy now . . . I mean . . . could you . . . show me around?" Her voice sounded very small.

She was rewarded by Greg's looking at her as though he had never really seen her before. "Sure! Maybe I can teach you to take over Tom's job!"

"Not a chance!" Tom laughed. "Who would help you with your chemistry homework between loads?" Tom and Greg both were majoring in chemistry at State College.

Greg groaned slightly, "That reminds me, we've got that big lab exam tomorrow." Then he led Sandra to the main brick building at the front of the plant. Without entering it, he said, "This whole building is where we do what we call finish work, the pressing and spotting. And that big barrel is where we store all the dirty spots we take out of the clothes."

Sandra knew that even a sophisticated guy like Greg expected her to giggle at his wit, but she just was not the giggling type. "We only do finish work during the day, though," he explained. Then he led her down the dark passageway to the shed.

Turning on a glaring fluorescent light, he said, "This is the washroom. Believe it or not, some clothes wash better than they dry-clean." Now he assumed a posture, bent with toil. Sandra liked Greg's occasional dramatic flourishes. "Many are the times I've been back here scrubbing my knuckles raw, while my dad sat up front smoking cigars!"

Sandra noticed a closet with a glass door toward the rear of the washroom. "What's that closet for, Greg?"

"Oh, that's the 'deadroom', where we keep all the unclaimed garments."

Sandra gazed at the pants and jackets and sweaters and dresses, which had once belonged to somebody. The sight made her sad, and she was glad when Greg switched off the light.

They returned to the cleaning room, where Greg explained to her a little about Tom's work. "I guess Tom has told you that we do all the dry cleaning in this building. The cleaning room has to be housed in an entirely separate building in our type of plant, because of fire regulations."

Greg showed her how the huge washers cleaned the clothes and how they were dried in big tumblers. Greg pointed to the tumbler Tom was loading, which looked to Sandra like a gigantic metal barrel. It measured about four feet in diameter and Greg told her it could dry two hundred pounds of clothes in one load.

"Tom better be careful how he treats that tumbler," Greg chuckled. "Oldtimers around the plant swear it's haunted."

"Haunted?" Sandra whispered. She knew there was something creepy about this place!

"The story goes that years ago a dry cleaner was working alone back here one night. After the tumbler had started revolving, he fell into it somehow. They didn't find him, until he had burned to death."

Sandra shuddered. The images the story created in her imagination left her speechless with revulsion. She noticed that Greg's brown eyes had turned black under his dark frown.

He shook his head slightly, then called to Tom, "Hey, I'd better get going."

"Yeah, let's try to get through early; I'd like to study a little more for that chemistry exam."

"Ditto!" Greg agreed. "By the way, don't forget to do the uniforms on the windwhip. See you later."

"I think I'd better be going, too," Sandy said to Tom.

"Yeah, Mom will be worried."

Sandra shook her head. "Patrick drove her to Glendale; she's baby-sitting overnight for the Fitzgeralds. And Kevin has a date," she added.

Tom looked up. "So no one's home, huh?" As she had hoped, he asked her to stay and keep him company, until Greg returned.

Tom had been fumbling with the on-off switch of the big tumbler. "Hey, Sam, bring me a flashlight, will you? There's one back there on the shelf in the washroom."

Even with Tom nearby, Sandra felt uneasy, as she scurried down the dark passageway. Groping for the flashlight in the dark, she felt sure someone was watching her. A tremor of relief slid down her spine when she finally found the flashlight.

Tom was standing by the switch box, which was outside the cleaning room on the dark side of the building. "Here, Sam, shine it up high." He opened the switch box and began checking each circuit with the fuse tester.

Sandra nearly groaned aloud each time he inserted the two-tined instrument. She didn't even realize she was shaking, until Tom complained, "Hold the light still! I'm almost through." When the little bulb on the fuse tester lighted once again, Tom shook his head. "Nothing wrong with the fuses."

Returning to the tumbler, he tried once again to start it. Getting no response, he walked toward the front building. "I'd better phone Greg at Peerless."

When Sandra followed him into the office, he was hanging up the phone receiver. "Now the phone is dead. Must have something to do with the storm, so I'd better drive to the gas station and try to phone Greg. If the buzzer rings, it'll probably be National Van Lines bringing in their furniture pads. Don't open the gate for anyone else."

"Why can't I go phone Greg?"

"Because he'll probably tell me what's wrong with the tumbler, and you'd get it all mixed up."

"Listen, Tom, I'm not going to stay alone in this creepy place."

"Oh for Pete's sake, Sam, don't be a baby! I'll lock all the doors, and you don't even have to open the gate for the Van Lines. Just tell the driver that I'll be right back!"

She sighed in resignation and didn't answer him. When she heard him drive off in her jalopy, though, she was overwhelmed with anger. "I'm sick of being taken for granted," she fumed. "Even Greg acts like he thinks the Kellys are four boys!"

She flopped onto a chair, buried her face in her hands and sobbed. When her anger had abated, the uneasy feeling returned. She longed to turn on another light in the dim office, but she could hear the storm blowing against the windows and couldn't force herself to touch the light switch.

Sandra frequently told herself it was fantastic, but she had been terrified by the possibility of being electrocuted, ever since a wintry day when she was seven years old. She and the boys had been confined to the house for several days because of a storm. Patrick, then thirteen, had become overwhelmed by boredom and suggested that they investigate the wine cellar.

They had a riotous time, tasting this and that, until they heard their mother's footsteps. The boys commanded Sandra, who happened to be on the basement stairs, to "Turn off the lights, quick!" When she touched the switch, a shock bit her hand. Then she had cowered on the stairs, whimpering, while the boys implored her to be quiet. When they had all been caught and punished, the boys had accused her of being a "sissy girl" and betraying them.

Now Sandra cocked her head intently. What was that noise? It was coming from the back of the plant. She held her breath as she strained to hear. Then she exhaled with a soft whoosh. She recognized the sound as the peculiar whirring the big tumbler made. "I've been so busy feeling sorry for myself,

I didn't even hear Tom come back," she thought half-aloud.

As she pushed her way between the racks of clothes outside the office cubicle, the garments seemed like lifeless shadows of their owners. She shivered and ran the rest of the way to the cleaning room.

In spite of the noise of the tumbler and the drumming of the rain on the galvanized roof, the plant seemed awfully quiet. "Tom?"

He must be here somewhere! Sandra felt panic swelling within her. "TOM! If you're hiding, it's not funny!" Her voice became plaintive, "It's too scary here!"

Then she remembered the locked gate. Unless she had opened it herself, Tom could not have come through the gate. And he had not come through the front building.

She was shaking now. Then who had started the tumbler? Suddenly she knew.

The dark alley leading to the washroom looked more foreboding than before, and the inside of the washroom was as black as a dark suit covered with grease. Her eyes had traveled along the darkness, fearfully, to the white shadow near the "deadroom." Sandra knew, though, that it wasn't a shadow.

Just a tiny sound escaped between her clenched teeth, but her brain was screaming. "The ghost! The dead dry cleaner started the tumbler!" She stared at his bloated shape, rocking silently in the air.

She backed away slowly, slowly, keeping her eyes

157

on the swaying ghost. When she reached the door to the front building, she whirled and ran. As she ran between the racks, toward the office, the lifeless clothes seemed to sway toward her, as though to clutch her with their limp handless arms.

Slamming the office door, she leaned against it, desperately trying to quiet her breathing. When she could inhale without gasping, she picked up the phone. "I'll call home. Maybe Patrick or Kevin is home now." The complete silence of the receiver against her ear reminded her that the phone was dead. She sagged against the desk, as limp as one of the shadowy garments.

Sandra jolted upright. She heard the dead dry cleaner calling to her. Then, if she hadn't been so sick with tension, she would have laughed. The ghost certainly wouldn't be so cruel as to call her Sam!

When she opened the gate for Tom, she felt more affection for him that she had in a long time. The feeling was short-lived, however, for he began scolding her. "Didn't you hear the buzzer? For Pete's sake, why are you running around with no coat on?"

The latter question was so unexpected, she stammered, "I . . . I . . . left my parka in the office."

"Well, go get it. Sometimes I think you're too dumb to come in out of the rain. I've got enough troubles tonight without looking after you."

"What are you so crabby about? You leave me here alone, where anything can happen, then all the thanks I get is being called a dumbbell."

"Thanks for what?"

"Never mind!" She felt like kicking him in the shin, but she strode away to get her coat. When she returned, she saw Tom unloading clothes from the tumbler, which was perfectly still, just as he had left it. Sandra forced herself to glance toward the washroom. It was empty. Not even a shadow resembling a ghost.

The uncertainty about what had happened or what she had imagined made her edgy. Therefore, when Tom asked her, as though they hadn't quarreled, to help him until Greg returned, she snapped, "I wouldn't be much help; I'm too dumb. I'm going home."

Without waiting for an answer, she let herself out the gate. In her car, she fished absent-mindedly for her keys through all her pockets, while her mind was full of the image of the ghost. "Oh darn it, anyhow." She felt like crying when she realized that Tom still had the keys.

When she reached the gate again, she stood in the rain, calling to him, as before. When he finally came to open the gate, he demanded, "How come you forgot the buzzer again?"

"Because I'm so dumb! Now give me back my car keys."

"I left them in the glove compartment." He strode away from her toward the cleaning room. Sandra couldn't resist the temptation to follow him and glance down the dark passageway once more.

There it was. The bloated shape of the dead dry cleaner rocked grotesquely in the same spot. Sandra screamed, "Tommy!" Through the thickness of her terror a crazy thought struck. She hadn't called him Tommy since she was twelve years old.

Then she heard a cry and a sickening thump. She whirled toward the cleaning room then staggered backward from shock. Tom had been caught from head to waist inside the tumbler, which had started to revolve.

She saw him nimbly draw his legs into the tumbler, then he braced both hands and feet against the walls of the revolving drum. But how long could he remain alive in there, even with the door open? Sandra's pulse seemed to keep time with the whirring of the tumbler, while her mind thrummed, How can I stop it? How can I stop it?

She jabbed at the on-off button which controlled the tumbler. Then she ran to the switch box which Tom had tested earlier. Grabbing the flashlight he had left nearby, she located the switch which she believed controlled the tumbler.

Sandra's hand reached for the switch, then stopped. She felt as powerless under the tyranny of her fear, as she had years ago in the wine cellar.

She leaned back and looked around the corner as the tumbler came down again and started another revolution. Tom hadn't made a sound, since he had fallen. The open door of the tumbler flashed by, and during that infinitesimal fraction of eternity, she glimpsed Tom's face.

Sandra was astounded. She was sure she had seen no fear in his expression. It was as though he was just waiting patiently for her to stop the tumbler.

She clenched her jaws so hard her neck hurt, then she grabbed the switch and pulled. The tumbler shuddered to a halt.

When Tom climbed out, Sandra was shaking more than he was. "Oh Tom, are you hurt?"

He leaned against her. "Not a bit, not even burned . . . just a little wobbly."

Sandra started to lean against Tom to steady her own shaky legs, then they heard the horn of Greg's truck in the driveway. Sandra stood erect and concentrated on looking calm.

She was pleased that Greg insisted on Tom's having an examination at emergency hospital. They compromised when Tom agreed to an examination the next day by his own doctor. Then he changed the subject by reminding Greg that they still had clothes to be dried.

Sandra left Tom and Greg working at the switch box, while she quietly investigated her ghost. Fearing their ridicule more than she feared the ghost, she forced herself along the dark driveway.

The awful shape still hovered in the washroom. Fumbling for the light switch, she propped up her sagging courage by reminding herself that she had pulled the tumbler switch.

She finally located the light, and the fluorescent glow flickered for a moment, then illuminated the entire washroom. Although she wanted to weep with relief, Sandra felt strangely disappointed. Her ghost, naked in the harsh light, was Tom's lab uniform.

It was hung above a windwhip, a device which

blew air and steam vapor into it from below. Thus, the bloated garment rocked grotesquely in the air, as though it were alive.

The story was so strange, she couldn't resist sharing it with Tom and Greg. Although Tom teased, he was gentle. "Darn it, anyway, Sam. I've been doing all the work tonight, and you've been having all the fun."

Sandra felt that Greg was half-serious when he said, "I'll bet there are a lot of ghosts around this old plant we don't know about."

"I still don't understand how the tumbler started and stopped by itself, though," she said.

When Greg took her hand, led her to the switch box, and explained the malfunction of the tumbler, Sandra felt that the whole frightening evening had been worthwhile. When he asked her if she knew what a conduit was, she knew it wasn't very feminine, but she did know. She answered, "A pipe which encases wiring."

"Right!" he exclaimed. "Well, we have a conduit running from the roof into the switch box. It has evidently got rain water in it, somehow, because there's water inside the box. When the water dripped onto the contact for the tumbler switch, it conducted electricity just as though a button had been pushed and the tumbler started. When the water dripped away, the contact was broken and the tumbler stopped. Simple, huh?"

"Oh sure," Sandra laughed. "Simple or not, it still scared me out of my wits when I was here alone."

"A wet conduit can cause all kinds of crazy things to happen. . . . Tom left you alone?" She felt a glow from head to toe, when she saw that he was looking at her the way Tom looked at his girls. "Tom shouldn't be so careless; you'd be hard to replace!"

They had returned to the cleaning room, and Tom laughed, "I have to admit old Sam does come in handy sometimes."

Greg turned to help Tom pull the loads from the small tumblers, in which they were completing the drying. Looking over his shoulder, he said, "Sandra, we're almost through with the cleaning. If you don't mind waiting a little longer, I know a nice, dark, pizza place. . . ."

"Now just a minute!" Tom interrupted. "Not unless I chaperone!" Sandra mentally blew a kiss to the whole haunted plant, when Tom added, "We Kelly boys are kind of careful about who goes out with Sandra."

There's No Stopping

Danny Dunn!

Danny Dunn, science fiction hero, with his friends, Irene and Joe, can't stay away from mystery and adventure. They have shrunk to the size of insects, traveled back in time, sunk to the ocean floor, and rocketed through outer space!

The DANNY DUNN books, by Jay Williams and Raymond Abrashkin:

_____ 44383	$1.95	DANNY DUNN AND THE SMALLIFYING MACHINE	#1
_____ 45068	$1.95	DANNY DUNN, INVISIBLE BOY	#2
_____ 44382	$1.95	DANNY DUNN, SCIENTIFIC DETECTIVE	#3
_____ 43877	$1.95	DANNY DUNN AND THE UNIVERSAL GLUE	#4
_____ 44340	$1.95	DANNY DUNN AND THE HOMEWORK MACHINE	#5
_____ 43404	$1.95	DANNY DUNN AND THE SWAMP MONSTER	#6
_____ 43678	$1.95	DANNY DUNN AND THE ANTI-GRAVITY PAINT	#7
_____ 43680	$1.95	DANNY DUNN, TIME TRAVELER	#8
_____ 43679	$1.95	DANNY DUNN ON THE OCEAN FLOOR	#9
_____ 43681	$1.95	DANNY DUNN AND THE WEATHER MACHINE	#10
_____ 43290	$1.95	DANNY DUNN AND THE FOSSIL CAVE	#11
_____ 47235	$2.25	DANNY DUNN AND THE VOICE FROM SPACE	#12
_____ 45753	$1.95	DANNY DUNN AND THE AUTOMATIC HOUSE	#13
_____ 44381	$1.95	DANNY DUNN AND THE HEAT RAY	#14
_____ 45754	$1.95	DANNY DUNN ON A DESERT ISLAND	#15

 POCKET BOOKS, Department ADD
1230 Avenue of the Americas, New York, N.Y. 10020

Please send me the books I have checked above. I am enclosing $_____ (please add 75¢ to cover postage and handling for each order. N.Y.S. and N.Y.C. residents please add appropriate sales tax). Send check or money order—no cash or C.O.D.'s please. Allow up to six weeks for delivery. For purchases over $10.00, you may use VISA: card number, expiration date and customer signature must be included.

NAME _____

ADDRESS _____

CITY _____ STATE/ZIP _____

876

☐ Check here to receive your free Pocket Books order form.

Do You Know WHICH WAY

To Go For Great Reading Adventures?

Go straight to these mystery and action-packed WHICH-WAY™ books—where **you** make the story go whichever way you want it to!

____ 45756	$1.95	**THE CASTLE OF NO RETURN #1**
____ 45758	$1.95	**VAMPIRES, SPIES AND ALIEN BEINGS #2**
____ 45757	$1.95	**THE SPELL OF THE BLACK RAVEN #3**
____ 43920	$1.95	**FAMOUS AND RICH #4**
____ 44110	$1.95	**LOST IN A STRANGE LAND #5**
____ 44189	$1.95	**SUGARCANE ISLAND #6**
____ 45098	$1.95	**CURSE OF THE SUNKEN TREASURE #7**
____ 45097	$1.95	**COSMIC ENCOUNTERS #8**
____ 46021	$1.95	**CREATURES OF THE DARK #9**
____ 46020	$1.95	**INVASION OF THE BLACK SLIME AND OTHER TALES OF HORROR #10**
____ 46732	$1.95	**SPACE RAIDERS AND THE PLANET OF DOOM #11**
____ 46731	$1.95	**TRAPPED IN THE BLACK BOX #12**
____ 50859	$1.95	**STARSHIP WARRIOR #13**

POCKET BOOKS, Department 2WW
1230 Avenue of the Americas, New York, N.Y. 10020

Please send me the books I have checked above. I am enclosing $_____ (please add 75¢ to cover postage and handling for each order. N.Y.S. and N.Y.C. residents please add appropriate sales tax). Send check or money order—no cash or C.O.D.'s please. Allow up to six weeks for delivery. For purchases over $10.00, you may use VISA: card number, expiration date and customer signature must be included.

NAME _____

ADDRESS _____

CITY _____ STATE/ZIP _____

☐ **Check here to receive your free Pocket Books order form.**

871